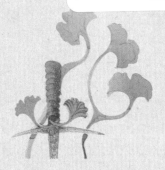

THE COWARD & THE SWORD

THE COWARD & THE SWORD

JUGAL HANSRAJ

ILLUSTRATED BY RUCHI SHAH

HarperCollins *Children's Books*

First published in India in 2021 by HarperCollins Children's Books

An imprint of HarperCollins *Publishers*

A-75, Sector 57, Noida, Uttar Pradesh 201301, India

www.harpercollins.co.in

2 4 6 8 10 9 7 5 3 1

Text © Jugal Hansraj 2021

Illustrations © HarperCollins *Publishers* India 2021

P-ISBN: 978-93-5422-846-9

E-ISBN: 978-93-5422-847-6

Jugal Hansraj asserts the moral right

to be identified as the author of this work.

Typeset by Pradnya Naik in EB Garamond 12pt/17.8

Printed and bound at Replika Press Pvt. Ltd.

MIX
Paper from
responsible sources
FSC® C016779

To my late Mum and Dad.
We live in eternal gratitude for all the
love you selflessly showered upon us;
enough to last us many lifetimes.
To Sidak – my very own Prince.

&

To my mentor – Daisaku Ikeda;
President, Soka Gakkai International

'A sword is useless in the hands of a coward'
- *Nichiren Daishonin*
(Reply to Kyō'ō, WND-1)

The moaning waters
Oragu Strait
Rainy Grove
rren desert
Kofu Army
Lumis Woods

KOFU

Kofu
Navy

Northern
Sea

Waki
Bay

Shonins
Cottage

Secret passage

MOLONGA

Nikato

The early morning light bathed the room in its warm glow. Prince Kadis got out of bed and walked to the window. He had never tired of the sight that met his eyes when he looked out. The white powdery sands of the beach far below him and the azure waters of the ocean beyond were starting to glisten like a million jewels. The boats of the hardy fishermen were bobbing up and down the waters, trawling for fish. In the distance, a few miles out further north into the ocean was a small island – the naval base of the Royal Navy and the vantage point for the sailors to keep watch over the Kingdom. And to the south, beyond the neatly laid-out gardens and the castle walls lay the capital city of the Kingdom of Kofu.

Perched atop a hill, this charming city was built along the slopes. A square in the middle, where the hill flattened out, played host to lively markets and a year-round festive atmosphere. Below the square, the hill continued to slope down until it reached a wall that marked the limits of the capital.

Beyond this wall lay some small villages and farmlands which stretched a few miles out on the plains. At the southern fringes of the Kingdom was a small, wooded forest and beyond the wooded area were the army headquarters and cantonments which were in place to protect the southern border of the Kingdom.

Prince Kadis, however, had never gone out of the gates of the capital city. He could only imagine the lands and the villages beyond because of the way his mother Queen Kanito would describe them to him. Her words would paint a vivid picture for him and through her he knew all about the Kingdom and the people that lived in it.

The King and Queen ruled over Kofu with love, compassion and kindness, doing their very best each day to make sure the people were looked after. Though they were royals, they didn't want to ever alienate their people and so they dressed in rich but simple robes – the King in deep burgundy and the Queen in soft cream shades. The sandstone castle was strong yet stark and their way of living simple. The people of Kofu made themselves useful in some way or the other and were a happy, satisfied lot. The King's guards and the Defence Ministry protected the little Kingdom – the army in the south and the navy in the north. The farmers tended the fields; the fishermen trawled the ocean for fish; the craftsmen looked after the welfare of all structures; the artisans made furniture, and kept the Kingdom filled with beautiful artefacts; and the musicians kept the culture alive along with the many others who contributed in different ways towards the smooth and peaceful running of the Kingdom.

Through his mother, Kadis also knew that though the Kingdom of Kofu was small and the people brave and

peace-loving, the neighbouring Kingdom of Molonga harboured ill will and jealousy towards his father, King Rissho. It was feared that these neighbours might even attack Kofu as it was rich in resources and very strategically located. King Rissho, though peace-loving, was also very wise. To that end, he had ordered his people to be battle ready. The ever-present war-clouds had prompted the brave people of Kofu to be prepared for battle at all times. It was a kingdom inhabited by the brave and the resourceful.

Well, with one exception: Prince Kadis, the young son of King Rissho and Queen Kanito. Kadis who would soon be a young man of sixteen years and would someday inherit the Kingdom to rule and look after. He knew in his heart that he did not fit in. That he was different.

That he was a coward.

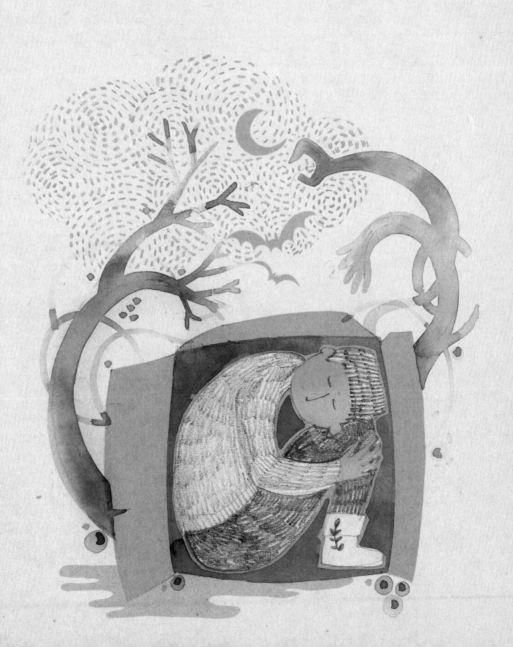

Young Kadis was scared ... of everything. Of stepping out of his castle, of meeting people, of falling sick, of playing sport, of training in warfare, and almost everything else imaginable. Kadis was a dreamer and was happiest staring out of his window at the ocean. He was a good-hearted young lad, raised lovingly by the King and Queen, who were both undoubtedly brave themselves. But Kadis lacked in 'character' if you went by an old saying in the Kingdom: 'A man with no skills, no bravery and no interests is a man of no character.'

King Rissho worried about young Kadis. All the young boys and girls born in the family down the generations had been brave and courageous. Rissho couldn't understand the cause of Kadis' fear and nervousness. He had everything at his disposal: he was getting a good education, the royal family was loved by all and it was a time of peace. But here was Kadis, a young coward, with no friends and no inclination to step out into the world.

As for the Kingdom's fragile peace, King Rissho often wondered how long it would last. The rumours were getting louder and his loyal band of informants spread out across the neighbouring Kingdom as spies had sent back discreet messages warning him of some rumblings of discontent and jealousy from Molonga, which

lay just a day's ride south of Kofu.

King Rissho decided to tour Kofu and travel to the cantonment in the southernmost part of his small Kingdom to check how the army at the border was faring. The army stationed there was building a long, high wall to make it more difficult for the enemy to attack.

The King was to leave on his journey the next morning along with his Minister of Defence and a small entourage of military personnel. On hearing his travel plans, Queen Kanito had a quiet word with Rissho. 'I've been thinking ...'

The King was all ears.

'Why don't you take young Kadis along for the tour tomorrow? Going out and living amongst the soldiers for a couple of days might give him some much-needed confidence and courage.'

King Rissho pondered over this for a while. Although there was peace in the kingdom, one could not rule out unforeseen trouble. Still, he was confident that his brave soldiers would fend off any attack. The young Prince would be safe by his side. King Rissho not only loved his son dearly, but he was also very concerned about him and yearned for the day when Kadis would take his duties as a Prince seriously and be like other boys his age.

'I think you're right,' he replied to the Queen. 'This tour might be a bit of an adventure for him as he hasn't ever ventured out that far. It could do him a world of good. Why don't you speak to him early tomorrow morning and get him ready and packed for the tour?'

'Yes, I will,' Queen Kanito replied.

Rissho was about to leave when his wife stopped him. 'I have another suggestion.'

King Rissho turned to her.

'You should also take along young Shijo. Having a companion of the same age might make it easier for our son. Send word immediately to his father.'

Young Shijo was the son of a farmer and was known to be a courageous boy. Despite being a commoner, Shijo's father was one of King Rissho's closest friends. Likewise, the King and Queen were happy to encourage a friendship between Kadis and Shijo.

'That's a good idea. I'll send word right away.'

And so saying, the King left to attend his court.

As word from the King soon reached the farmer, he called for his son and gave him the news. Shijo of course readily agreed to join the King and his entourage on the trip. He respected the royal family too much to say no, and young Shijo was always up for an adventure. He too had never visited the army cantonment at the far southern limits of the Kingdom. So, he was quite excited to go!

Prince Kadis and Shijo had met several times as their fathers were good friends. Kadis liked the company of Shijo but due to his own nervous and anxious nature he hadn't really pursued a friendship with the farmer's son, nor for that matter the friendship of any other young boy or girl in the Kingdom.

The following morning the King, his Minister of Defence and their entourage were ready to leave. Shijo had woken up early and had met the entourage well in time for the journey. Just being part of the excursion was a dream come true for him. He felt overawed yet excited to be standing there with the royal castle as a backdrop. He looked around him and eagerly took it all in. King Rissho looked very regal as he discussed some important matter with his minister. The Royal Guard were in their positions, the carriages looked luxurious and the horses were all primed to begin the journey. However, Kadis was nowhere to be seen.

Inside his room, Queen Kanito was busy persuading him not to be afraid of the journey.

'No, mother! It's ... it's too far south ... and I don't want to be away from home ... what will I do there? And besides ... I'm frightened!'

'But son ... I can't understand why you wouldn't want to go. There's nothing to be afraid of. Your father is an accomplished warrior and is riding through his own Kingdom with his Minister of Defence as well as five soldiers of the Royal Guard, the small elite force trained to protect our family at all times. You'll be safe and well protected.'

But the young Prince clearly did not want to join his father on the tour.

'No ... I ... I don't want to go!' Kadis cried out.

But the Queen continued. 'Kadis, my dear,' she said gently, 'this trip will be good for you and you must see the kingdom that you will one day inherit and meet the folk you will be responsible for. And Shijo will accompany you.' After some quiet deliberation, Kadis reluctantly agreed. Queen Kanito helped him pack and get ready. The King and his entourage were waiting.

As King Rissho saw his son approach, accompanied by Queen Kanito, he remembered the old adage that his uncle had taught him as a young boy – 'A son that can fill his father's shoes and not just follow in his footsteps but someday surpass him, will make his father a very proud man.' He hoped Kadis would one day be just the son to make not only him, but his mother and the entire population of Kofu proud.

King Rissho was pleased to see Kadis dressed in his official robes, looking every bit the Prince that he was. Seeing the royal crest on one side of his son's tunic and the symbol of the crown on the other made the King very proud. It wasn't often that Kadis agreed to wear the official robes and tunic.

Though delayed by over an hour, the King and the entourage were happy to have the Prince join them on the tour. And so began the journey that was to change young Kadis' life forever.

03

The entourage left the hilly capital's winding and cobbled streets. As they passed through the city gates, all the citizens cheered and waved at their beloved King and at the Prince who they hardly knew. To them he was the reclusive royal. Not many knew of his nervous, shy nature or even that he had been rather reluctant to join this trip. Young Shijo on the other hand was very excited and honoured to be part of the excursion. For him it was a once in a lifetime opportunity to see the entire Kingdom, and with the King, at that! Once they had toured the southern border and stayed there for a few days, the King planned to return to the castle for a short rest before taking a tour of the neighbouring little island at the northern end of his Kingdom to review his navy's war readiness.

King Rissho was hopeful that this trip and Shijo's company would help Kadis come out of his shell.

Shijo and Kadis were in a separate carriage right behind the King's. Kadis was gloomily looking out of the window when he heard Shijo's voice.

'Prince Kadis, how often have you been to the army camps in the far south?' Shijo asked enthusiastically.

'Never ... this is my first time,' Kadis replied flatly.

'Never? I'm surprised to hear that. If I may ask ... how come?'

The Prince sighed, 'I've seldom stepped out of the castle grounds and on the few occasions I have, I've only ever been around the hilly capital town and never gone beyond its walls. Today is the first time I'm venturing out of the capital's gates. The first time in my life actually.'

'But ... but it's your Kingdom! Don't you ever feel like touring the villages and meeting all the people?'

'Well ... I do feel like stepping out sometimes but ... I don't know how to explain ... I'm not sure you'd understand ...'

And with this, Kadis just sighed and noticing Shijo's look of concern, gave him a weary smile. He then went back to looking out of the window of his carriage.

As they passed the small villages, Kadis could see how much the citizens of Kofu loved their King. They held them all in such high esteem, including the Prince. Kadis realized with a growing sense of alarm that the responsibility his father carried so ably on his broad shoulders would be his one day.

At nightfall, the King and his party stopped at the last village that lay just before the small forest. Beyond it lay the army camps and the southern border. The council chiefs lived in the largest houses in the village and often played host to royal visitors. All the warm hospitality and respect afforded to the royal entourage made Kadis even more uncomfortable.

The village council chief had planned a grand feast to welcome them to his home. It was not often that this village at the far end of the Kingdom had the honour to host the King himself. The council chief and his wife were gracious hosts. They were happy to meet their nephew Shijo and gave him a warm welcome. Just before the feast for the royal party started, the chief respectfully leaned over to the King and pointed to the young girl standing in front of them.

'Your Majesty, I would like to introduce my daughter Sara.'

King Rissho smiled warmly at her as she bowed and shook his hand confidently.

'Pleased to meet you, young lady.'

Sara was a beautiful, self-assured girl. She had a soft and pretty face with fiery brown eyes and lustrous, auburn hair. She wore her beauty lightly and was dressed in a simple but smart gown for the feast. Shijo and Sara already knew each other as they were cousins, but Sara was happy to meet the rest, including the strange and shy Prince. King Rissho made the introductions.

'Sara, meet my son, Prince Kadis.'

Kadis hesitatingly shook her hand. Sara gave him a friendly smile which put him slightly at ease. He looked around the crowd and slowly retreated into a corner.

As Sara and Shijo walked away after everyone had been introduced, Sara leaned over to him and whispered, 'He's certainly not what I thought a Prince would be like!

I've never met anyone so quiet and reticent.'

Shijo nodded in agreement. 'Yes, that's what I thought too. He seemed a little sad. But I guess I would be sad too if I didn't have any friends. But although he's shy, he seems to have a kind and gentle disposition.'

'That's the feeling I got. Anyway, I'm glad to have made his acquaintance,' Sara said happily.

In the course of the evening, the King was greatly impressed by Sara's views on the kingdom. The chief was a bit nervous when Sara started voicing her opinions as he wasn't sure she knew how to be diplomatic. But the King felt she was a smart young lady who was refreshingly honest. He even thought her opinions and suggestions had merit.

Young Kadis, however, found the girl to be quite strange. Behind her angelic face lay quite a passionate personality and she was unlike any girl he had ever met.

When the feast ended, King Rissho said, 'Sara, I would like to invite you to join us on our tour of the army camp and be our guest at the army cantonments.'

Sara couldn't believe her ears – an invitation from the King himself! King Rissho turned to her father. 'With your permission, of course. It's only half a day's ride from here and I assure you she will be well looked after.'

The council chief readily agreed. What an honour for young Sara. On her part, Sara was very excited to be part of the entourage and happy that she would get to know more about the shy Prince.

04

The next morning the royal party bade the council chief and his wife adieu and made their way out of the village. They soon entered the forest beyond which lay the southern border of the Kingdom. The densely packed, tall forest trees made Prince Kadis edgy and instead of staring at them in wide-eyed wonder like Shijo and Sara, the young Prince slid into his carriage seat, drew down the blinds and stayed inside until they had passed through the forest canopy. Even though he was surrounded by his father and a few royal guards, Kadis was scared and tense as they journeyed through the forest.

Finally, they emerged from under the forest canopy. In the distance, they could spot the army cantonments and the big wall that was being constructed there. The wall was an imposing sight indeed! It extended from the foothills in the east to those in the west. The camp itself was laid out like a grid and the soldiers that manned the camp looked disciplined and battle ready. The army General, on spotting the royal party, galloped across on his horse to greet them. He escorted them to the royal camp that was set up for the comfort of the royal party. They were to rest for a bit and then the army General and a few important officers would escort them on a tour of the army camp so the King could get an idea of how the preparations were progressing.

Being this close to the southernmost border made Prince Kadis very uncomfortable. He had heard whisperings in the castle that the King of Molonga was planning an attack. If they did attack, it would be through this very border. Even though his father had a well-trained army, the Prince was anxious at the thought of something going wrong. As he was lost in these thoughts, a very excited Shijo and Sara entered his tent.

'Prince Kadis, I've never been around so many soldiers. This is all very thrilling!' said Sara with a twinkle in her eye.

Shijo too couldn't control his enthusiasm. Instead of sharing in their excitement, Kadis said unhappily, 'There's nothing to be so happy about. I would have much rather stayed in the comfort of my warm room at the castle, staring at the beautiful blue ocean. Being so close to the border is quite a frightening prospect!'

'My dear Prince, there's absolutely nothing to be afraid of. You have the entire army to protect you.'

But Kadis looked at them and sighed gloomily. Shijo and Sara didn't know how to comfort a Prince that they were barely acquainted with. A few minutes later, they could hear some activity just outside the tent. A royal guard came to request they step out as it was time for their tour.

As scheduled, the army General escorted the royal party on a tour of the entire area. The rest of the day was set aside for this very purpose. All the soldiers were very honoured and encouraged by the visit of their brave King. They had been looking forward to seeing the Prince for the first time but when they finally met him, they were slightly disappointed by his timid nature. In a few years, it would be the Prince who would lead them into battle if it so came to pass, but he didn't quite inspire the same kind of confidence in the army that the King did.

They soon came to the foot of the big wall. The wall was mostly ready, save for one section to the far west. It was a most imposing structure and looked nigh impenetrable. Kadis, Sara and Shijo looked on in awe. When it came time to climb the steep steps to the top of the wall where the archers were positioned, Kadis refused. The King and his retinue were to go all the way to the top to meet the brave archers, but the Prince was afraid of heights. Sensing this, King Rissho took his son aside and whispered firmly, 'You don't have to be frightened. I'll be right ahead of you through the entire climb. Besides, it wouldn't look too good if the future heir to the throne was scared to climb to the top of the very wall which is meant to defend his own Kingdom.'

Very reluctantly, and because he was rather intimidated by his father's imposing personality, a flustered Kadis agreed to join him and the rest of the party up the steep stairway that was constructed on the Kingdom side. King Rissho and the General led the way, followed by the royal guards and then by Shijo, Sara and a very scared Prince. As they started the climb, fear was written all over the Prince's face. A few soldiers dropped what they were doing and came to the foot of the stairway to see the shaking Prince climb the steps with great hesitation and fear. Shijo and Sara didn't know what to make of this strange predicament. They weren't yet close enough to the Prince to take the liberty of comforting him. As they continued the climb, Kadis stopped about a quarter of the way up. His father, the General and the guards were almost at the top by now. But Kadis just couldn't take another step. He froze on the spot the moment he glanced down and saw how far up they had reached. A few more soldiers gathered at the foot of the stairs to witness this awkward scene. Thus far they had always heard and known the royal family to be full of brave men and women. The sight of the Prince frozen with fear was a strange sight. Seeing the soldiers gather below, Sara felt a wave of sympathy for poor Kadis. She leaned towards him and whispered, 'Prince, please try not to look down ... look straight into my eyes instead.'

She discreetly held his hand. 'Please continue to look at me and just follow me up the stairs.'

Kadis did as he was told and started his climb, looking into Sara's eyes as he moved forward. Kadis had never seen such fiery eyes on such a gentle face. It was also the first time a girl had ever held his hand. Kadis was transfixed and before he knew it, he was standing

at the top of the wall. The soldiers down below cheered encouragingly. King Rissho was filled with pride on seeing this and it put to rest his doubts on whether it had been a good idea to bring the Prince along on this journey. 'The company of young Shijo and Sara will be a good influence on Kadis,' he thought happily. Meanwhile, Kadis was now worried about the climb down.

As they followed the King across the top of the wall, a strong wind started to blow. The wall was quite long and went up to the other end of the foothills, the last part of which was scheduled to be completed in a few weeks' time. The top of the wall was only wide enough for two soldiers to stand side by side. King Rissho was very impressed with the arrangements and all the archers were honoured to have him

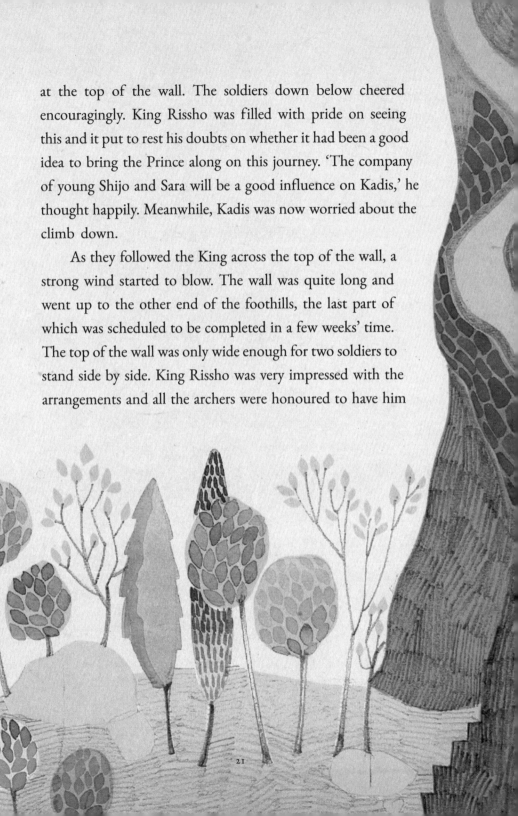

in their presence. The army General led the royal party to the centre where they stood directly over the part of the wall that had a big, heavy gate at the centre. Shijo and Sara turned around towards the Kingdom and urged the Prince to do the same. The entire Kingdom of Kofu lay in front of them. It was a majestic sight indeed. Kadis was awestruck. Surrounded by mountains on both sides, Kofu looked magnificent. It was a tiny Kingdom but a beautiful, prosperous and happy one. But, the thought that was uppermost in Kadis' mind was: would he ever be able to protect this charming little Kingdom? 'Why can't I be as brave as my father? Or even as brave as Sara and Shijo, for that matter?' he thought unhappily.

Soon it was time to go all the way down the steep, narrow stairway. As the royal party began their descent, Kadis froze again at the top of the stairs. He had looked down and the height was too imposing. As vertigo began to kick in, he panicked and his knees started to wobble. Sara tried to take control of him but this time to no avail. The Prince felt woozy and everything started to spin around him. Beads of perspiration formed on his forehead and in a few moments, he passed out. Sara and Shijo held on to him as the royal guards came running to assist them.

⊷ 05 ⊶

When the Prince came to, he was already at ground level and in the safety of the Royal tent. Shijo and Sara were sitting close by along with King Rissho. 'It's all right, son,' he said gently to reassure his son, but this only made Kadis feel worse. Kadis was mortified that he had let his father down in front of the entire army.

It was dark outside now. A guard entered and whispered something in the King's ear. Patting his son's head, King Rissho got up to leave, saying he had someone to meet. Shijo and Sara followed soon after as they wanted Kadis to get some rest. Alone in the tent, Kadis' mind was a maze of thoughts as he wondered why he couldn't be like everyone else. 'Why was I born a coward?' he thought sadly. Suddenly he heard some voices behind his tent. 'Who is father speaking to?' he wondered. Curious, he went over to the back of his tent to listen to the conversation.

Kadis raised the flap of the tent and gingerly stepped out into the shadows. There he saw a white-bearded elderly man of regal bearing walking towards his father. Though he was dressed in austere brown robes, he had an air of nobility about him. King Rissho hastened towards him and bowed respectfully. From their conversation, Kadis learnt that the elderly man was Shonin, the King's uncle—the brother of Rissho's father; and Kadis' granduncle—a relative he had never even known he had. Shonin had an impressive personality and a deep baritone voice. Kadis further gathered that his granduncle Shonin lived just outside the southern limits of Kofu, in the land beyond where the wall was being constructed. His father had requested an audience with him and his uncle had very graciously offered to come see him. He had also wanted to see his grandnephew. They spoke briefly about some disagreement that had taken place many years ago between Rissho's father and Shonin. Kadis didn't know what the disagreement was about but it had been bad enough to have caused a lifelong rift in the family.

Shonin had since moved away from the castle and was now living a simple, almost ascetic existence in a small cottage in a forest about a mile away from the army cantonment area. The King asked Shonin to move to the capital city of the Kingdom so that he would be protected in the event of an enemy attack. But old Shonin refused politely, saying he was happy where he was and that was the end of that. King Rissho, though disappointed with the refusal, respectfully invited Shonin to enter the tent to see his grandnephew. On hearing this, Kadis lifted the flap and quickly retreated into his tent.

When Shonin and King Rissho entered the tent, Kadis was already under his woollen blanket, pretending to be asleep. Shonin's towering presence filled the tent. He walked up to the sleeping Kadis and looked at him for a long while, not saying a word. It was almost as if he was reading the aura around his grandnephew. He then turned to King Rissho,

'With your permission, please may I have a moment alone with my grandnephew and give him my blessing?' he asked.

For some reason that Kadis couldn't fathom, Shonin's deep voice was as comforting to him as a cup of warm cocoa. King Rissho smiled graciously and left the tent. Kadis was facing away from his granduncle. Shonin smiled and spoke aloud even though Kadis was presumably asleep.

'I'm leaving one of my horses behind. He's a stately, old, grey

horse and goes by the name Greybeard. If anyone should ever need to speak with me, my horse would lead him straight to my cottage ...'

Kadis couldn't understand why his granduncle would say such a thing to a sleeping young lad. Shonin then came closer and said in a low voice, that was almost a whisper,

'And son, getting to my horse one hour before midnight would be a good time!'

It was an intriguing message for Kadis. Shonin left without another word.

Long after he was gone, his presence still filled the space within the tent.

After a while, sensing he was all alone, Kadis got out of bed. The rumbling voice of his granduncle still filled his ears. Kadis couldn't understand why Shonin wanted to meet him at the cottage. It was pitch dark. The tent next door belonged to his father who was probably fast asleep by now and the tent on the other side of him housed Shijo and Sara, who were likely to be sleeping too. Even though Kadis was afraid of the dark, a voice in his head was telling him to go to Shonin's horse and have him lead the way to Shonin's cottage. Kadis finally gave in to this annoyingly persistent voice. He stepped out of his tent as silently as he could and looked around. A royal guard was stationed there. He instantly stood up on seeing Kadis, who pretended to take some deep breaths, gestured towards the tent of Shijo and Sara and hastily made his way there. The guard presumed the Prince wanted to be with his friends. All the guards by now knew of his nervous disposition.

Kadis entered his friends' tent and stood there in the dark for a few moments wondering what to do next. Shijo and Sara—sensing someone there—turned on the gas lamp. Much to their surprise they found the Prince standing in their tent, looking very tense indeed. They immediately jumped out of bed and went to his side. Kadis had never had any friends before but he found these two very comforting and dependable to be around. He trusted his instincts, a first for him, and sat down on Shijo's bed. The two cousins sat down beside him and asked what the matter was. Kadis took a deep breath and told them about his granduncle, a relative he never knew he had for his father had never mentioned him in all these years. And then he told them about Shonin's horse, and how he felt strangely compelled to go meet his granduncle. 'I think Granduncle Shonin wants to speak with me urgently,' he added.

Shijo sat up excitedly. 'Gosh ... This sounds just like a minor adventure!'

He was always up for one, however major or minor it might be. Sara too looked eager at the prospect of giving the guards the slip and following the horse to Shonin's cottage. A secret rendezvous with an old royal was enough to whet their appetite for adventure. They encouraged the Prince to go with his gut and to meet the old man. Of course, Kadis was afraid of slipping past the safety of the guards, stealing out from the gap at the far end of the wall under construction and following his granduncle's horse to a cottage about a mile away from the safety of the army cantonment.

It was just a few minutes away from the 11th hour. The trio lifted the flap at the back of the tent and looked out. The guards were discussing the next day's schedule with the Minister of Defence and did not notice young Shijo and Sara leave their tent, along with the Prince. Taking advantage of the darkness, the three stealthily made their way to where the horses were tied. Some distance away, the old grey horse stood by himself, as if awaiting the group to come by. And come by they did, with Sara taking the lead, for she was the least afraid of the three. Sara went up to Shonin's horse, patted his neck and untied him from the fence. The stooping Greybeard was instantly alert as if he was expecting just this and swiftly turned and started walking away. Kadis looked at his companions. They gestured to follow the horse. Under cover of darkness, the horse took them on a roundabout route towards the far end of the wall, to the small gap which would be completed in a few weeks. Once the wall was complete, the only way in and out of Kofu would be through the massive and heavily guarded gates. The grey horse led

them to the far side near the gap in the wall. But, instead of leading them through it, straight to the four guards on duty there, he led them to the thick bush at the edge of the hillside. The Prince did not like that at all. He was about to protest when Sara firmly clasped his hand in hers.

'We are going to meet your granduncle—not some stranger—so, trust him,' she whispered with a smile. Her voice and her hand in his reassured him.

They walked through the thick foliage for a while. The horse then led them through a small arch created by the bending of trees, which framed the entrance of a cave. Greybeard bent his neck and pointed to something on the ground. Sara stepped forward to have a look. It was a thick tree branch with a cloth tied around one side. Next to it were some matches. She immediately understood what needed to be done and lit a flame on the dry tree branch, so that it could serve as a torch. The horse entered the cave and the rest followed. The torch threw up wobbly shadows on the rough cave walls. A flurried Kadis stayed close to his friends as they walked out of the other end of the cave and pushed through a thick wall of rough undergrowth that led them out into open fields. It was quite likely that the soldiers didn't know of this secret passage through the trees.

Once they were out in the open, dark plains stretched out in front of them for a few miles, extending right up till the hills in the distance. Beyond the hills were the passes through which the enemy would have to approach. Molonga was but a few miles beyond these hilly passes. From the wall, there was a clear view of the plains

and the entrance to the passes, so the soldiers of Kofu would be
well prepared in case of an enemy attack. But old Greybeard had
no intention of leading them into the hills and passes beyond. He
turned sharply into another wooded area.

As they moved forward, Kadis was filled with a growing sense
of unease. Shafts of moonlight penetrated through the leafy canopy
of the tall trees, creating an eerie pattern of shadows and moonlight
on the forest floor. His mind started to play all sorts of tricks as he

heard unseen night-time creatures in the dark. He shut his eyes tight and asked his friends to turn back, but they were so excited with this little escapade that they didn't heed his warnings. The Prince now had no choice but to go onwards with them or head back by himself. Since the latter was certainly not an appealing option, his teeth began to chatter, which they often did when he was ill at ease. It was as if they had a mind of their own. Shutting his eyes tight did bring some relief.

Soon, the woods opened out into a clearing. And in that clearing stood a small wooden cottage with a thatched roof. The chimney had a welcoming spiral of smoke coming out of it. It seemed warm and inviting. Greybeard stopped by the door. The trio stood outside the door wondering what to do next, when a booming voice rang out from within.

'Kadis, Shijo, Sara! The door's open!'

❧ 07 ❧

Filled with trepidation, they slowly opened the antiquated, heavy wooden door. In the middle of the dimly lit room, on a large, worn leather chair in front of the fireplace, sat old Shonin, smoking a well-used curved pipe. His warm, welcoming smile put them instantly at ease. When Shonin stood up, he towered above them. He ushered them into his simple cottage, which was more befitting of a humble village artisan rather than royalty. They sat down on the mismatched wooden stools around the room, a bit unsure about why they had come here in the first place and what they should say or do now.

'I knew you would come, Kadis ... and I also knew your friends Shijo and Sara would be the ones to bring you here.'

The three wondered how Shonin knew Shijo and Sara's names but didn't dare say a word. Shonin smiled as if he could read their minds. 'You don't need answers to all your questions,' he said with a mischievous smile.

'You must be wondering how you haven't heard about me yet,' said Shonin as he stood up and went to the stove where some hot soup was bubbling away.

He poured out three welcoming cups for the hungry adventurers.

'Your grandfather—the great King Nara—was my older brother.

He was as brave as the legends narrate; bravery runs in the family,' he said, looking at Kadis.

Shonin went on to narrate how although both he and his brother were brave, they had different ideas of bravery. King Nara had the ambitious streak of a conqueror, but for Shonin, bravery meant keeping peace with their neighbours. To create peace when war was looming upon them was the act of real bravery. It was easy to attack, or to defend with weapons, but it took real courage to go out to the enemy and extend a hand of peace, letting go of all pride and ego. That was not something King Nara agreed with. Thus, the two ideologies clashed. Shonin, who wanted to tread the path of peace, was branded weak and a coward. He voluntarily decided to exile himself and lead a peaceful life away from politics and war, both of which he detested. Not many of the new generation even knew if Shonin was alive, or of his relationship with the royal family.

Kadis and his friends were astonished to hear this history of the royal family which they had no idea about. There was silence for a few minutes before the young Prince cleared his throat to speak. 'Sir ... I mean *granduncle*, you said everyone in the family was brave and that our family was known for our courage ... but you see ... not everyone ... I mean ... I know that I'm not brave at all ...'

Shonin put his hand up and smiled warmly. 'Admitting that you're not brave is the bravest act of all, my child! It takes a person of great courage to admit that. Even the bravest and most powerful Kings don't have the courage to admit their shortcomings. That, in fact, makes you a very brave person indeed. Now that you know your weakness, you have to find the resolve to overcome it. That is

what makes a man or woman of great character.'

He looked at the young Prince's friends, 'And your two new friends, they both have real courage too. I can see it in their eyes. Especially Sara ...'

Sara blushed. Kadis took a deep breath and was about to ask a question when the wise old man interrupted him, 'You want to know about your grandfather, I'm sure.'

Kadis was surprised how the old man knew. Shonin walked up to a massive old wooden chest in the far corner of the room. The chest creaked and groaned as he opened its heavy lid, like it hadn't been opened for a long, long time. He bent over and lifted an item that seemed heavy and was covered in an old dark cloth. He carefully wiped the dust off and placed it on the centre table. By now he had the complete and undivided attention of his audience. He smiled at the trio as he lifted the cloth and revealed an old sword that must once have been magnificent.

The trio looked on in wonder at the heavy, unwieldy weapon that had clearly seen better days.

'Let me tell you about the legend of this sword. This might come as a surprise to you but at one point in history, the Kingdoms of Kofu and Molonga were united. It was one big Kingdom!'

The three friends were surprised to hear this. This was something they had not been taught in their school. Seeing their expressions, Shonin realized that their curiosity was piqued, so he continued. 'Molonga was a state or province of the Kingdom of Kofu and was governed by Prince Honji, who was a cousin of mine and my brother King Nara. We later learnt that Honji harboured ill-will towards Nara as he thought he should have been King of Kofu. Of course, Nara was the rightful heir to the throne and did a great job of ruling the Kingdom, but Honji was envious, he resented all the credit that your heroic grandfather King Nara would walk away with every time Kofu won any wars. Ego and greed led him to believe that he himself would make the better King, though we all knew that he didn't rule his province of Molonga very efficiently. Many a time my brother would have to send me there to undo the mess he created. He was more interested in the position and power than the responsibility that came with it. What he didn't realize was that when a person fulfils his duty honestly and efficiently, success

KOFU

MOLONGA

38

and recognition most certainly follow ... but you can't have the recognition without doing your duty first. This resentment festered and grew in the heart of Prince Honji.'

The three friends were so enthralled with the history lesson they were receiving that their soup remained untouched and had gone cold. Shonin proceeded, 'There came a time when Nara got news that a King at the far end of the peninsula was planning an attack on Kofu. He asked Honji to keep his army in Molonga ready as that would be the first point of attack by the enemy. But Honji had other plans. The enemy attacked the province of Molonga first, as Nara had predicted, but for the first time the army at Molonga was outsmarted and the enemy progressed to face Nara's army. After a long battle, Nara not only drove the enemy back to their Kingdom at the far end of the peninsula, but he also launched a counter-attack, razing their entire Kingdom to the ground and taking control of their treasures. I supported the decision to defend our Kingdom but didn't approve of Nara chasing the enemy down and routing their Kingdom in return. Anyway, your victorious grandfather King Nara came back with vast treasures.'

Shonin lit his pipe and continued, 'The next day Honji arrived asking for the treasure to be equally divided between King Nara and himself. Considering his army had been defeated and he had let the enemy succeed in attacking the capital of Kofu, he had some nerve. Later that night, King Nara got to know that Honji had played dirty, and it was he who let the enemy into the province of Molonga by stealth, and deliberately led his army to the wrong gate. Some of his own soldiers were killed as he had to show that he really had attempted to defend his province. Then with Honji guiding the enemy King, they had reached the gates of the capital. Fortunately, Nara was a brave leader and had been prepared for the enemy attack. Honji had planned that once Nara was defeated, he would sit on the throne and in return give a considerable reward to the enemy for helping bring King Nara down. So, it was our own cousin who betrayed Kofu and the King. Upon learning the facts, Nara was so livid that he himself went to the province of Molonga and confronted Honji, who of course denied the entire incident. This led to a bitter argument and a scuffle ensued where Honji drew his sword to attack his own cousin, the King!'

The three friends were speechless. The story had carried on deep into the night but the friends were way past caring about such trivial matters as a good night's sleep.

Shonin continued, 'Now let me tell you about this sword that was drawn by Honji. The sword was a family heirloom and upon becoming governor of Molonga, Honji had expressed a desire to be gifted the sword. This sword was very precious to Nara as it was a symbol of Kofu pride and had passed on to Nara from our ancestors. But King Nara was big-hearted and Honji was family after all, so he gifted it to him on the condition that Honji would care for it with great pride and allow Nara to see the sword whenever he visited the province of Molonga. Honji of course believed that owning the sword made him more powerful so he started getting ideas of being King himself. When the fight broke out between the cousins, it was his intention to use the sword to kill Nara and take possession of the throne himself as he knew that I wouldn't be interested in laying claim to the throne. But while defending himself, Nara got hold of the sword and in the scuffle Honji got killed by the very sword that he intended to kill the King with. An angry Nara stormed out of the stately royal home and took the sword with him. But the death of Honji caused a lot of strife and Honji's family demanded that they separate from Kofu and get their independence.

'After a lot of tension, struggle and even violence on both sides, Nara got fed up and granted Molonga its independence. But ever since then, the Molongans, especially Honji's son Toki, refused to believe that it was his father who betrayed Kofu or that it was Honji who had first tried to kill King Nara and thus died in the ensuing fight. He now wants to wage war on Kofu and get his talismanic sword back, even though it was King Nara's to begin with, and kill King Rissho. Luckily his daughter Tara is of the new generation and from what I know, she is peace-loving and wants nothing more than to unite the two Kingdoms and families.

'Anyway, soon after, my brother King Nara fell ill and passed on the Kingdom to your father. Just before he passed away, he entrusted the sword to me as it reminded him of the animosity between the families of the once united Kingdom, so he didn't want it in his possession anymore. After he passed away, his son King Rissho ruled in a slightly more peaceful manner but still didn't let go of his feelings of mistrust towards Molonga. I tried to visit Molonga and broker peace between the two Kingdoms but instead, I was branded weak by the council of ministers and told that I had no place amongst the brave soldiers of Kofu. I started to realize that I did not belong here anymore. Nor could I go and live in Molonga as

I was considered their enemy.

'King Toki wanted to bring down Kofu and started to secretly build up his armies. Ostracized by both, I decided to live in neither kingdom and was content to live out my remaining years in self-imposed exile in the woods outside the fringes of Kofu. I took the sword with me. I did keep getting news from the Kingdom thanks to my few trusted followers and that's how I heard about you and how you were different from the rest of your family. My heart went out to you and under the guise of meeting my nephew, I actually came to meet you. I had a feeling you would understand what I had to say about our history.'

Everyone was quiet for a long while. Shonin lifted the sword and brought it close to the young Prince.

'This sword is now yours, my child!'

09

Kadis couldn't believe what he had just heard. Only a few moments ago, Shonin had been talking about peace but now he wanted his grandnephew, who was anything but brave, to have the sword that once belonged to the Molongans. The sword that was a symbol of the animosity between the two Kingdoms. This seemed very strange indeed. As if reading his mind, Shonin smiled understandingly. 'Don't be surprised, my child. I know how much this old, dull looking sword was feared many years ago. But the might of this sword depends on the one using it. It can be used for either peace or war, it's up to the person holding it.'

Kadis was now quite afraid to have the much feared and legendary sword so close to him. 'But granduncle ... I know nothing of peace and war, nor of any of the politics involved. And ... and this sword ... how can I ... how can I use it for peace ...?'

Shonin smiled mysteriously. 'Oh, but you can! Remember the history that I just narrated, and understand that how you use this sword is up to you.'

'But can't you see granduncle, I'm not brave. How can I use this sword?'

Shonin patted Kadis on his shoulder and said something that the young prince would never forget all his life.

'A long time ago, I learnt something from a very wise sage: A

sword is of no use in the hands of a coward.'

'But ... but ...' Kadis tried to protest.

Shonin persisted, 'The braver you get, the more useful the sword will be for you. Think of it like magic. You see how dull the blade of the sword is, so also the bejewelled hilt of this once magnificent sword. The greater the courage in your heart, the shinier the sword will become! Here, keep it, it belongs to you – you're the one destined to inherit it.'

'But ... but what am I going to use the sword for? How can I create peace from a weapon that was used to cause so much destruction? How, granduncle ... *how*?'

Shonin smiled warmly again, 'That, my boy, is completely up to you! It is your destiny now. Use it for peace or use it for destruction: it's your choice. Be brave and use it wisely. And don't be afraid to keep it simple ... sometimes that's the best course of action.'

So saying, the old man walked to the door and opened it, letting in a waft of cold breeze into the warm room.

'My trusted horse Greybeard will lead you back to the army camp the same way you came. And keep Greybeard with you. He's yours to look after, and I can assure you that he will look after you too.'

He ushered the trio out with the parting words, 'But do remember the words of the wise sage from long ago ... A sword is of no use in the hands of a coward!'

Shonin gently shut the door and a moment later the light inside the room went off. The three friends suddenly realized how dark and cold it was. Shonin's horse neighed and started to walk ahead. The trio had no choice but to follow, this time with young Kadis carrying his destiny and the destiny of the two warring Kingdoms with him ...

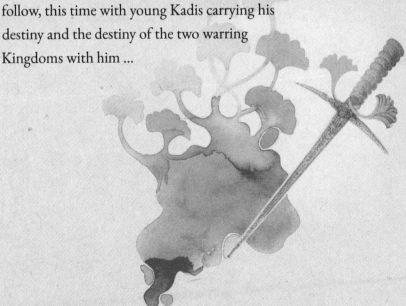

10

Safely back in the warmth and comfort of his tent at the camp, the young Prince was grateful to old Greybeard for stealthily bringing them back without alerting the royal guards. 'That old horse is a wise one indeed,' he thought to himself. Kadis carefully hid the old sword among his belongings as his friends had suggested. Once they were back home, they would help him decide the next course of action.

The next day, King Rissho and his entourage, satisfied with the preparations they had seen at the army cantonment and with the construction of the wall, started their journey back to the capital of Kofu. For the night, they stopped at the village where Sara lived. They were once again given a warm welcome by the council chief and his wife with another big feast prepared in their honour. King Rissho, who was very impressed with young Sara, asked the council chief, 'May I have your permission for young Sara to join us in the capital? Sara could train there with the civic administration and someday hold a position of importance. We most certainly could use someone as smart as young Sara.'

Sara blushed. The chief and his wife were ecstatic on hearing the King's praise.

'Your Majesty, we'd be happy and honoured to send Sara to work at the castle. I know she would love to go,' said the council chief, looking at his daughter with great joy.

King Rissho was happy at their decision.

'She will be my responsibility hereon and I will make sure she is well taken care of.'

For some strange reason—a reason he couldn't quite fathom—young Kadis was very pleased with this development.

The next evening, the royal party was back at the castle. King Rissho was quite happy with the growing friendship between Prince Kadis and his two young companions. He admired their character and fortitude and felt their company might bring about a positive change in young Kadis.

A few days later, Sara started her training with the Civic Administration Department and Shijo was offered a place to stay within the castle grounds, so he could remain close to Prince Kadis as well as accompany him for his scholarly lessons and weaponry training to become a warrior. King Rissho felt Kadis might take to the training much better if he had a friend with him. And this way he would help another young lad from his Kingdom get a great education and improve his life. Pleased with the arrangements, King Rissho left for a few days to tour the seafront in the north of the Kingdom with the Naval Admiral.

Sara's living arrangements were also made within the castle grounds in a small cottage by the castle gate, so it was easier for her to go for her training every morning. The three became close friends and soon formed a circle of trust. One misty evening, a few days after the King's return, Shijo and Sara were sitting by the window in the young Prince's apartment when Sara brought up the topic they had all brushed under the carpet. 'What's to be done with the legendary sword, and what of the talk the wise old Shonin had with us?'

They now had a different perspective on the history of the Kingdom and on war itself. Like Shonin, over the last few days they had come to hate all that war stood for. But how could they stop these erstwhile friendly and related Kingdoms from going to war?

The three friends sat together by the fireplace sipping cups of cocoa and discussing ideas. Then Kadis took a deep resigned breath and said, 'I can't figure out what old Shonin was trying to get us to do. I mean, the only idea we haven't come up with is to just waltz into the Kingdom of Molonga with a whistle on our lips, ask directions to their King's castle, saunter in and hand him their symbol of pride, this old sword of theirs and pass on an imaginary message from my father that the show's over and you can have total control of your Kingdom back, give them a goodbye hug and end years of hostilities in an instant!'

Shijo was impressed. He said excitedly, 'You know, Kadis, actually, that would be the best plan ever – if only we had the courage to do it!'

Kadis shrugged. He had only meant this as a joke.

Sara was quiet for a few moments and then spoke up, 'You know, I really don't think anyone can come up with a better plan than this to get rid of all this enmity, this strife between two peoples who are so similar and so related to each other. As Shonin told us, "Sometimes, keeping it simple is the best option." Don't you remember?'

Kadis walked up to the old wooden wardrobe where he had

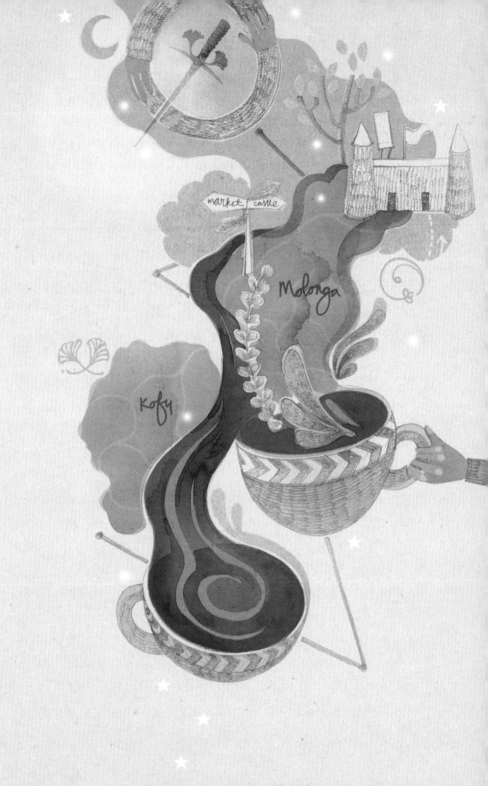

hidden the sword. He bent over and picked it up, placing it carefully on the table. He unravelled the dark cloth and there it was: the once magnificent sword, now a lacklustre blade with a dull handle. He hesitatingly put his hand around the hilt and lifted the sword. It weighed a ton. He had been training with swords but this one was different; it was much too heavy and one would have to be very brawny to use such a weapon. Sara walked up to him and asked,

'Just *how* brave would you have to be to be able to use this sword?'

Kadis sighed, 'Well, I guess I would have to be very, very brave indeed! Brave enough to let go of all my fears, and change the impossible ...'

Kadis stopped short and held his breath. Just talking about bravery made the dull sword emit a faint glow. 'It feels a tad bit lighter now, and the handle fits just a bit more snugly in my hand!' he said excitedly.

As a small edge of the blade started to shine through the dullness, Shijo jumped up.

'It's just like old Shonin said ... a sword is of no use in the hands of a coward. By the same theory, the braver you get, the more useful the sword will be!'

Sara couldn't believe what she was seeing. Old Shonin wasn't trying to trick them, he meant what he had said. She went up to Kadis and urged him to repeat the plan he had mentioned in jest. And as Kadis spoke of the plan (that he hadn't really believed in to begin with) the sword got a bit lighter, the blade just a tad bit shinier and the jewels on the hilt just that bit more radiant.

'Oh my goodness!' exclaimed Sara. 'It's almost as if the sword is agreeing with us.'

None of them had ever seen anything like this before. It was a magical, mystical moment. And then Kadis spoke up, as he normally would, 'B-but even if it is a good plan ... how can we ... h-how can I of all people go ahead with it? I mean, walking into enemy country, p-putting our lives in danger ... and firstly, how would I ever get permission from my father to do that?'

As he rambled on nervously, the blade of the sword dulled again, the jewels lost their sheen and the blade became heavy. His grip in which the hilt had started to fit a little bit better, suddenly seemed too small for the sword.

Sara pointed to the sword, 'Look ... look how it went back to its old state the moment Kadis started to feel nervous.'

Shijo whispered under his breath, 'A sword is of no use in the hands of a coward ... *this* mystical sword is of no use in the hands of a coward. Old Shonin even hinted that to keep it simple is the best thing. And your plan is brilliant in its simplicity.'

Kadis put the sword down and looked at his friends.

Sara took a deep breath. 'Well, at least now we have a possible plan. But do we have the courage and the faith? And secondly, how do we convince our King that we need to leave the safety of Kofu and walk into Molonga?'

The three friends were in quite a quandary. They now knew what they had to do. The question remained, how would they do it?

◆§ II ◈◈

The next couple of days were spent going about their daily duties and the three never mentioned the 'plan' or how to implement it. They were each lost in their own thoughts. *Peace.* If only they could meet Shonin and seek his help. Kadis shrugged and muttered to himself, 'I know granduncle Shonin called upon us to perform the near impossible task of bringing peace between the two Kingdoms and ending the prospect of war once and for all. If only I had his wisdom, experience and valour.'

Later that evening as the sun was setting, Kadis and Shijo made their way to the private dining hall of the castle where they were to have dinner with the King and Queen. Sara was to join them too. This was a weekly ritual King Rissho had started to keep track of the progress the trio were making in their respective fields of training. He of course had a special interest in seeing that Kadis was training to be a brave young man and a capable heir, in spite of his weaknesses. Besides, he had taken a liking to young Shijo and Sara and was happy at the flourishing friendship and trust that was steadily building up between them. He hoped that by helping Shijo and Sara who both had a fine character, he would be encouraging two young and capable people in his Kingdom. And he could already see that they were a good influence on his son.

Sara met Kadis and Shijo in the courtyard and as they started to make their way in, they were suddenly stopped in their tracks. An old horse cart was parked outside. They recognized it immediately – they had seen it outside Shonin's cottage in the woods. This could only mean one thing: Shonin was here! It was as if their wish had been granted. They glanced at each other and hurried in.

As they entered the hall, they saw King Rissho seated at his usual place at the head of the table with Queen Kanito by his side. Across from them sat old Shonin. They were deep in conversation and Shonin's impressive voice filled the hollow, empty space of the stark dining room. On seeing Kadis and his friends, King Rissho stopped mid-sentence and stood up. He was always happy to see the three together. He walked up to them and greeted them warmly. The Queen gave the three an affectionate hug. She was so happy that her reticent son now had some true friends. King Rissho looked at old Shonin and then at Kadis, and said, 'Son, I'm sorry – but I haven't ever spoken about or introduced you to my uncle, your granduncle.'

As if on cue, Shonin stood up, almost filling the vast space and smiled a warm smile through his big white beard. Kadis was about to say they had met him when Shonin's heavy voice put a halt to anything that the Prince might have wanted to say.

'I did see you a few days ago but you were fast asleep then. A pleasure to finally make your acquaintance, my young Prince of Kofu!' said Shonin with a mischievous wink. Their meeting at the cottage was to be a secret. Kadis caught himself and smiled back formally. He walked up to his imposing granduncle, bowed respectfully and then shook his hand. The King didn't catch the impish smile the Prince gave his granduncle in return. He then gestured to his three favourite people to take a seat. With their hearts beating wildly, the three tried to make sense of Shonin's sudden appearance at the castle after all these years of self-imposed exile – it was almost as if he knew of their predicament.

As they all adjusted themselves in their seats, King Rissho spoke up, 'Son, I'm seeing my uncle here at the castle after many years. Several years ago, my father and uncle Shonin had a difference of opinion which I don't want to go into. Due to those differences, Uncle Shonin decided to leave all matters of state to my father; he retired into the forest and has been living a quiet life for many years in a small cottage there. He did come out of his self-imposed exile to attend my father's funeral but he has mostly been away. Whatever differences they might have had, and whether I agreed with his ideology or not, I have always held my uncle in the highest esteem. I learned a lot from him in my youth, and the person I am today has a lot to do with my time spent with him before he went away to lead a solitary and ascetic existence. Many a time I was tempted to seek his advice but knowing his stance on certain matters and out of respect for his privacy, I refrained. In fact, when we were touring the southern fringes of our Kingdom, I had sent him a message requesting he allow us to move his cottage to the capital of Kofu. Uncle Shonin had visited me at the camp to personally refuse my request. Though I know that he primarily came there to meet his grandnephew whom he had never seen, let alone met. But you were ... er ... indisposed due to your tiring day at the wall and were fast asleep. I didn't have the heart to wake you.'

Kadis shifted in his seat, as did his two friends as they recollected their small adventure into the woods to meet old Shonin at his cottage. King Rissho continued, 'Actually, it was *I* who requested an audience with my uncle, and it was *he* who offered to come to the castle today, a gesture I truly appreciate.'

The young Prince was now really curious; from the time he had entered the hall he had thought that old Shonin had come of his own accord, as some kind of mystical answer to their prayers. But now it seemed, he had been summoned by the King.

'A few nights ago,' King Rissho continued, 'as I was preparing to sleep, I mysteriously found a handwritten note from my father. It was written many years ago, in fact just before you were born. In the letter my father, who was ailing at the time, said that he respected

his brother immensely even though they had taken different paths. He had branded him a coward for his ideology, but in his heart he believed in Shonin's courageousness. As King, he had to listen to his Council of Ministers and whatever happened was as a result of that. My father was distressed by the situation. He also wrote that he was aware of my as-yet-unborn child. He stated explicitly that he would like nothing more than that his grandchild, the young Prince or Princess as the case may be, be sent to live with their granduncle in his cottage as soon as they turned 16 and be under his tutelage. He considered his brother very wise in most matters other than the politics of state and wanted our child to get an education, so to speak, from wise Shonin. I am, however, at a loss as to how that letter in my father's own handwriting and with his official seal came to be found after all these years.'

At this very moment, Shonin cleared his throat and when the three young friends turned to look at him, he discreetly winked at them. It was Shonin's doing! Kadis couldn't figure out how he had done it or made it happen, but he was certain that old Shonin had something to do with the letter.

King Rissho continued, 'As I have always obeyed my father's wishes and especially since this was as good as his last wish, I have decided to send you to live with uncle Shonin to help build your character.' He looked towards his uncle and went on, 'Even though I might not agree with his opinions on matters of state.'

Shonin just shrugged nonchalantly, 'My opinions on state matters will not be imposed on the young Prince's education.'

The King nodded in grateful acknowledgement. 'Thank you,

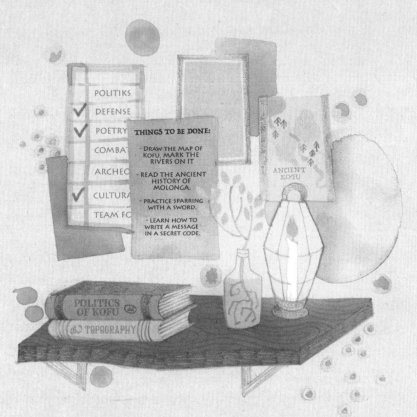

uncle. However, I am concerned about the Prince and his friends living in a cottage outside the wall. I would like to propose that you move inside the Kingdom, preferably within the castle grounds or the capital city itself, but otherwise at least to one of the towns or villages of Kofu.'

After some deliberation, Shonin said, 'Fine. I agree to move to a cottage provided by you within the wall but on one condition.'

King Rissho listened intently as Shonin continued, 'My condition is that my new cottage will be right at the border, by the far westerly side where the wall is being completed, at the edge of a cluster of trees. That way the young Prince and his companions will be inside the safety of the wall, inside the safety of the Kingdom, close to the army cantonment area but I'll still be able to maintain my privacy in my cottage by the woods.'

Kadis understood the reason and so did his friends. That cluster of trees hid the secret way out of the Kingdom. King Rissho nodded.

'Very well. I have a condition too. In case the Molongans do attack and their army is spotted approaching the wall, my soldiers will immediately evacuate these three youngsters from the cottage and bring them to the safety of the castle.'

'You have a deal,' Shonin readily agreed with a smile. If his plan worked there would be no need for an evacuation as there would be no war.

King Rissho smiled and respectfully bowed. 'So it's settled then! I will arrange for a new cottage to be set up and your things shifted inside the Kingdom's borders within the next few days. And then next week I will send Kadis, Shijo and Sara to you after we've celebrated my son's 16th birthday.'

12

A sumptuous banquet was held to celebrate the 16th birthday of Prince Kadis. The banquet hall was decorated in a grand and tasteful way. The royal cooks had gone out of their way to ensure that the food at the banquet was both exotic and delicious. The best musicians were invited to perform, and they did so with all their heart, for they had the highest regard for the royal family. Smaller feasts were planned that same evening in all the villages of Kofu so the entire Kingdom and its populace could be a part of this momentous occasion. Queen Kanito had outdone herself with preparations for this banquet.

The guests were pleased to see the handsome young Prince. But they secretly wished he had inherited the bravery of the royal family. Kadis looked anxious in the presence of so many people and tried several times to leave discreetly, but was thwarted each time when his father would call out to him to meet some prominent person from the Kingdom. Shijo's parents were there too, as were Sara's, the latter delighted to see their daughter glowing with happiness. It was a grand evening and the King and Queen had gone all out to make it a memorable one as Kadis and his friends would soon be away for several months to stay with Shonin.

On seeing how uneasy Kadis was around the crowd of people at the banquet, both Shijo and Sara decided to stay close to him all evening. Kadis did feel comforted by having them around; Shijo

FELICITATIONS PRINCE KADIS

even whispered in his ear, 'You better start getting a bit braver my friend, for what we might have to face will be a lot more challenging than hobnobbing with friends and family!'

At the mention of their possible adventures with Shonin, Kadis squirmed in his seat. For him just going to live in a cottage with a granduncle he barely knew, and that too at the far edge of the Kingdom—more than a day's ride from home—was adventure enough. But, for some reason he found strength in the presence of Shonin and in the company of his two most trusted friends.

Two days later, it was time to pack for their trip. The Prince's anxiety had reached a new high. He was ruing the day he agreed to this entire adventure.

13

Soon the day of the trip arrived. It was a beautiful morning. The sun was shining brightly, birds were chirping and Kofu seemed a cheerful place. But our poor Prince Kadis was anything but happy. It was time to bid adieu to his mother and father, who were standing by the royal carriage which was to take the trio to the far edge of Kofu. The carriage driver would also serve as their security guard till they reached there, although the three young adventurers were sure to be safe and welcome anywhere within the Kingdom. The carriage was soon on its way and with a one-night stop planned at the home of Sara's parents, it would be a pleasant journey.

After a fortifying hot meal and a good night's sleep at the council chief's cottage (for all except the anxious Prince), the trio awoke and were ready to embark on the last leg of their journey to Shonin's cottage. Once they crossed the woods, an army patrol would escort them to Shonin's door. Shonin had requested the King to not have any guards around the cottage, as he wanted the kids to have as normal an environment as possible so they could freely go about their education – a condition to which the King readily agreed as the wall was now complete and the army cantonment just a short ride away. In fact, Shonin's cottage by the trees was just at the outskirts of the army camp. Beyond the trees were the foothills of the impregnable mountains.

Or so the King thought. He had no idea of the passageway to the outside.

In fact, no one had any idea of that passage through the mountain.

As they disembarked from the carriage, old Shonin was outside his door, awaiting their arrival with a warm smile on his kind face.

The cottage was similar in style to the one they had visited earlier, but far newer and in much better shape. And it was a lot bigger too. But the old man didn't seem too happy with the arrangements though one couldn't see exactly why. The cottage had three extra rooms for the friends to sleep in. Kadis' room was in the middle and faced the front and not the woods behind the cottage, which was a comfort for him. Shijo and Sara's rooms were on either side.

They soon tucked into the hot stew that Shonin had kept ready for them. Shonin then asked them to settle in and rest in their rooms. They would speak the next day after breakfast.

The next morning at the breakfast table while Shonin made them some fresh bread and fried eggs, he told them that he would start their lessons from that day itself. He didn't mention any plan to stop hostilities between the two Kingdoms, nor did he say anything about the sword. Every night at bedtime Shijo and Sara would discuss how they would bring it up the next morning, but in Shonin's intimidating presence they became tongue-tied. Prince Kadis was quite happy to be receiving an education on the detailed history of Kofu, on the geography of the surroundings, on statesmanship, the art of diplomacy and many other subjects that a young royal assuming positions of importance would need. Shonin had immense knowledge to offer and the first two weeks they spent there were very interesting for the three friends. The progress they made in this short time was better than a few months at their school within the castle walls.

14

One morning over a bowl of oats and fruit, Kadis' wise old granduncle leaned in and whispered conspiratorially, 'As you can see, the guard stationed discreetly to monitor your progress has been called off! He has reported to the King who seems happy with the arrangements and security of the area.'

The three friends had no idea that they were being watched by any guard. Shonin continued, 'So what have you thought of my plan to create peace between Kofu and Molonga? Would you have the warm comforting rays of peace or the dark gloomy clouds of war?'

The three friends nodded in unison, 'Peace, of course!'

'So, then I would need three very brave young soldiers to make that happen ... and I happen to know just the three!'

'Er ... *brave*, you said?' Kadis interjected.

Shonin smiled and adjusted his spectacles, 'Yes, *brave* ... and by *brave* I mean *you* three!'

Kadis gulped in fear while his friends couldn't hide their excitement.

'When you go to war you need big imposing-looking soldiers, an army and all sorts of frightening-looking weapons. But when you maintain peace, what do you need? Since peace is the opposite of war then what you need is just the opposite. Three young innocent friendly faces that mean no harm to anyone. Therefore, just like you have soldiers of war, you also have soldiers of peace. Which is what you will be.'

The three friends exchanged a quick glance. Shonin continued, 'When you send soldiers to war, they are a threat to everyone who crosses their path. In turn, the people across them mirror what they see and become threatening in return. But on the other hand, if a soldier of peace, carrying offerings of friendship, bows in respect and asks everyone to forget the past and begin anew and offers an important gift as a symbol of peace ... what happens then?'

Sara spoke up straight away, 'You get a bow of respect from the person in front of you, just like a mirror image.'

'Correct!' Shonin was happy with the response.

'See, now that's the ideal way for things to happen. But it's not that simple. Because of so many wars and all the threatening and brandishing of weapons all around, it will take some time for the mirror to be polished as it has been muddied with all the bad stuff. So, when you meet them with respect, at first they'll suspect some kind of trick, but if you're sincere, then they'll realize that you're really there for peace and to make friends.'

Kadis thought about this for a while before speaking up. 'But granduncle ... you mentioned the word brave ... surely you can't mean me ...'

Shonin adjusted his spectacles and smiled warmly. 'There you go again! Well, everyone says you're timid ... a coward, even ... but you, my young Prince, are here, aren't you? If you were indeed as fearful as you think you are, you would have never made the journey here. You see, your problem is that you want to be brave but something

inside is telling you otherwise. All you have to do is tell that voice inside you that it is wrong. And that you are very brave because your intentions are noble, and you mean well. How can you be a coward if your intentions are so lofty? Something for you to think about, my young lad ...'

Kadis tried to say something when Shonin interrupted him, 'And don't forget, you have the sword with you.'

Kadis gulped, 'Sword? You don't mean *the* Sword? I know nothing about swords, let alone the magical sword itself!'

Shonin smiled affectionately. 'Boy, do you even know what's magical about that sword? At the risk of repeating myself, let me tell you again. The braver you get, the more useful your sword will be. It's all up to you, my boy. Bravery and cowardice are two sides of the same coin. Now, which side you choose ... is completely up to you ...'

Shonin got up and walked up to the sword. He unveiled the old, dull blade and placed it on the table in front of them.

'Now we will start the real training. If I took this sword and walked into Molonga, people would recognize me and at once assume I was there to create some sort of trouble. On the other hand, no one knows you and where you're from. This will work to your advantage. You must reach the King of Molonga and present your case. Now bravery is not only about brandishing a sword and cutting off people's heads; anyone with a little bit of training can do that. True bravery is the opposite of that. It is being brave enough to create friends out of enemies.'

The trio listened with rapt attention.

'To begin with, I will teach you the geography of Molonga and the history of the enmity between our two Kingdoms. The wall in our kingdom is being built to protect Kofu, but that will only create more suspicion and hatred. We must stop this now.'

For the next few weeks Shonin put all his heart into teaching them in detail about the history of the two Kingdoms and what had transpired between them. How they had gone from being close allies to becoming sworn enemies. He taught them the lay of the land, the customs, the traditions, and all that he knew about the Molongan royal family. King Toki of Molonga had a young daughter named

Tara, about the same age as the three friends. Maybe they could somehow talk to her and get a way in.

One evening as they sat together listening carefully to Shonin, they heard a squawking sound and Shonin instantly got up and rushed out of the back of the cottage. Intrigued, the three friends followed. What they saw astonished them. A majestic peregrine falcon with sharp talons and large, wide wings was perched on Shonin's forearm. Though it was quite an intimidating creature, it was very docile in Shonin's company. Shonin petted it affectionately. The bird had a brass ring around one of its claws to which was attached a small scroll of paper. Shonin pulled out the paper and smiled warmly at the big bird who promptly flew away into the trees with a loud screech. Shonin rolled open the little parchment to read it. Then without saying a word he went back into the cottage.

Inside, he lit the fire in the fireplace and sat down. He was deep in thought. The three friends waited patiently for him to say something but it felt like an eternity before he finally spoke. 'I've just received some disturbing news. The army of Molonga is preparing for war. I have some trusted spies planted in the Civic Administration Department of Molonga. They have just sent me this message. Your father has no knowledge of my source of information, though. My informant tells me that the Molongans have gathered their forces in large numbers and are planning a major attack on Kofu. What was until now a strong rumour has been confirmed.'

'But, sir, I'm very sure the armies of Kofu will quash their efforts!' Shijo spoke up with a certain degree of patriotic pride.

Shonin shook his head. 'You see, that's not the point. Who

quashes whom, who wins the war ... all these are useless questions. There will be grievous loss of life, property and many other important things on both sides. I could very well send word to King Rissho about the imminent attack and he will be ready to crush the enemy army. But what is the point of that? War will still happen. We must stop this madness before it begins. To enjoy our own lives, we need peace, not only in our own lands but also around us. I will have to advance my plans of sending you there. I'll send word first thing in the morning with my falcon and have my informant meet you and get you inside Molonga. He'll know the best way. And then you must get in touch with the Princess there and seek her help. But first win her trust! After that it's up to you. I can only get you in and provide you with all the information. The rest I will leave to your own ingenuity. Get a good night's rest. Tomorrow morning, we pack, and I send word. And tomorrow night, under cover of darkness, you must leave with Greybeard as your guide. Go on and get a good night's rest.'

But rest was the last thing on Kadis' mind as he thought anxiously of their trip into the enemy Kingdom as spies. On the other hand, Shijo and Sara couldn't quite contain their excitement. They were going to be soldiers of peace and go down in history. They were filled with optimism while the young Prince found himself under a heavy cloud of doubt.

The majestic falcon soared in the air, circling the cottage a few times before landing on Shonin's arm. It was almost noon. The falcon had returned with a message from Shonin's spy in Molonga. Shonin read the little parchment carefully and a few moments later a smile broke out on his lips. He turned and walked into the cottage without a word. The three friends had been staring out of the window at Shonin and quickly looked back in when he entered the room. Shonin paced up and down for a few moments and then said, 'I've received word from my informant. We're in luck! He was overseeing a cadet training group which was returning from a hike. There are about a hundred of them, plus the few helpers that he has with him. Three more young cadets will go unnoticed if we play our cards right.'

Kadis' palms became sweaty.

'Er ... and if we don't?'

Shonin smirked, 'We'll find out soon enough, won't we now!'

The Prince gulped in fear. Shonin patted him on the shoulder. 'When you begin any adventure, optimism is the quality that will make the difference between success and failure. Keep that in mind, my young Prince. You'll thank me later.'

He then turned to all of them.

'So off you go to get ready! You leave after sunset. If anyone can make this happen it will be you. And don't you worry about a thing. My trusted informant there goes by the name of Mr. Joi. He will make sure no harm comes to you. You're in safe hands,' he said with a twinkle in his eye.

He then reached into his pocket and took out an odd-looking whistle.

'Whenever you need to send me a message, use this whistle. My trusted falcon will always be somewhere close by and will come to you. Attach your message inside the brass ring on his claw and I'll get it soon enough.'

Soon they were ready to leave. Their bags were packed and the sword had been hidden away safely among their belongings. It was a beautiful night with the stars twinkling brightly in the night sky. There was only one last thing left to do before they set off on the journey of a lifetime: to give their mentor Shonin a tight hug, partly out of affection and partly out of a need for comfort. Shonin affectionately embraced his three young disciples. As a parting shot he told them, 'Your father will not know of anything till he hears of the success of your mission. I'm as proud of you three as I'm confident of your success. Go forth and make new friends and create a legacy of peace and happiness in the region for all of us!'

Shonin's trusted horse Greybeard then led the carriage away. As the cottage receded into the distance, the trees on the wooded foothills came into view and in a short while they entered an area completely covered with a thick canopy of branches and trees. Soon after, Greybeard stopped and turned. They had reached the entrance of the secret cave

housing the tunnel they were to go through to reach the other side just before dawn. From there a short ride would lead them to the spot where Mr. Joi was to meet them. Sara lit the two torches and handed one to Shijo and kept the other for herself. She went up to the front of the carriage closer to the horse while Shijo stayed inside the carriage with Kadis, who was quite afraid of the dark.

'I suggest you have a good rest while I keep watch,' he assured Kadis.

The young Prince was comforted by Shijo's words and after a few anxious moments, drifted off to sleep. Shijo placed the torch on the holder outside the carriage window and though he tried his best to stay awake he soon drifted off to sleep too. Sara heard the two snoring and shrugged. She was quite fearless so she decided to take control and make sure they stayed in sight of old Greybeard, who was a few paces ahead of them.

Kadis awoke to the sound of birds chirping. He opened his eyes to find that they were out in the open and the sun was slowly starting to rise, spreading a warm orange glow across the sky. He turned to find Shijo fast asleep with his head resting on the window frame of the carriage, and the torch snuffed out. He shook Shijo awake and leaned outside to find Sara sitting alert and in charge of their one-horse carriage, a few paces behind Shonin's trusted horse. At that very moment, Greybeard stopped and turned towards them with a neighing sound.

Sara halted the horse carriage and turned around to check on the boys. She smiled on seeing the young Prince looking quite radiant in the morning light. 'Good morning lads! I guess old Greybeard is trying to tell us it's time for some breakfast before the last leg of our journey. We've made good time but must eat fast so we can reach the spot before Mr. Joi arrives.'

After a good breakfast, which Shonin had thoughtfully packed for them, they followed Greybeard to a secluded spot at the foot of a hill. The area was dense with shrubbery. Shijo and Sara got out of their one-horse carriage to wait for Mr. Joi. Kadis remained in the relatively safe confines of the carriage. Soon after, they heard a shuffling sound and a short, stout, balding man emerged from the shrubbery, looking pleased to find the carriage already there. Shijo and Sara were immediately on their guard as they had never seen Mr. Joi, though the person in front of them matched the description that old Shonin had given them. The jolly-looking man walked up to the two of them and introduced himself as Mr. Joi. Kadis also tentatively stepped out of the carriage to meet the newest participant in their adventure. Was this really Mr. Joi and could he be trusted, Kadis wondered worriedly. He whispered to Sara, 'What if this is not Mr. Joi but someone else who has gotten wind of our plan to enter Molonga?'

Sara tried to reason with Kadis, 'But who else would know of

this plan? I'm quite convinced this is the right person.'

Kadis shook his head. 'Hmmm, I don't know really ... what if ...' but he was interrupted.

A familiar voice boomed from behind the shrubbery, 'There you go doubting again! That is indeed the same Mr. Joi I wanted you to meet.'

The three friends turned around and to their extreme surprise they saw emerging from the shrubbery none other than old Shonin himself. They rushed to hug him, elated to meet him out here in the middle of nowhere.

'But granduncle ... how did you ... where ... I mean how come ...'

Shonin laughed as he looked at the relieved face of his grandnephew, 'My little Prince! Do you think I would send you all the way to a foreign land on a dangerous mission such as this with no intention of keeping watch over you?'

Sara was perplexed. 'But we never saw you the entire journey ...'

Shonin said with a smile, 'My child, I do have some talents that you three might not know of! While you are on this bold and brave mission, I will always know where you are and what you're doing. You will never be alone. Just close your eyes and think of me and either I myself will be there, or some sort of help will reach you. Keep the faith, my young ones.'

Seeing their visibly relieved faces, Shonin continued, 'Mr. Joi is my most trusted informant. He has been living in Molonga as one of them for many years now and knows the entire Kingdom and all the important things there. He has a little network of reliable spies himself so you will be well looked after. Now Mr. Joi will help you join the ranks of the cadets and smuggle you back through the border of Molonga. Once inside, he will whisk you away to a safe house close to the capital where you will await further instructions.'

The next instant, the sound of falcon wings made them all look up.

'Oh, and another thing,' said Shonin, 'as I had told you, my trusted falcon will also be keeping a close and discreet watch over you. So you see, my young Prince, though you may think you're in this alone, so long as you have faith in the righteousness of your mission you will always be protected.'

Young Kadis was quite relieved to know all of this.

'So off you go with Mr. Joi, and good luck, my soldiers of peace! Return the legendary sword to the King of Molonga as a symbol of goodwill and let us put an end to this prolonged war of many, many years!'

Safe in the knowledge that they were being watched by the wise Shonin, they set off. Their carriage followed Mr. Joi, who was on his horse. Old Greybeard plodded along behind them this time. After a short ride, Mr Joi stopped the small caravan and dismounted.

'So now, you see, the rank of cadets will be filing up here for a short break before the last leg of their hike back to the gates of Molonga. As they rest and regroup, you see, they will all set off, with me keeping close watch at the back of the ranks. That's when I'll signal to you three to join the end to make up the last row of cadets. All my trusted team members are in charge of the cadets, you see, so they will deliberately miscount and let you in, counting the number of cadets as 100 when actually it will be 103! Once in, you see, there will be another short break where we'll present the cadets with a certificate of honour. At that time, you see, I'll whisk you away in my carriage to the safe house, you see. All clear?' The three soon noted that Mr. Joi had a habit of saying 'you see' after every few words.

Sara excitedly jumped up. 'Yes, we see!'

They soon heard the sound of feet scrambling up the nearby slopes, accompanied by loud commands. 'Halt! At ease, cadets!'

Mr Joi looked at his young wards. 'You see, those are the

voices of my trusted team members. Once the cadets have had their refreshments and get up to resume their hike, we'll join them at the back. And now it's time to bid old Greybeard goodbye. This is where he leaves us and heads back to Shonin to await your return.'

Mr. Joi looked at Greybeard and nodded. Nodding back, Greybeard turned and started to walk away. Kadis was sad to see the old horse go, and hoped he would see him again soon. Mr. Joi then handed the trio some uniforms.

'Please put these on, you see, and make them appropriately messy and please look suitably exhausted!'

The three quickly changed into their cadet gear and threw themselves onto the muddy ground and began to roll around. Mr. Joi slapped his head. 'I said "suitably messy", you see, not like you've been through a dust storm!'

Kadis, Shijo and Sara had a good laugh. Shonin's surprise visit had helped put Kadis at ease and he was actually beginning to have a good time.

As the cadets stood up and regrouped, Mr. Joi discreetly went up to the end of the ranks and signalled to the three friends to join him. They came out of the shrubs and slowly joined the back of the ranks of the young cadets of Molonga. Kadis observed that the young cadets in front of them looked a lot like they did. They were all just young, innocent teenagers doing their duty. He wondered what the point was of warring with them when they all looked and seemed so similar.

They soon approached the border check post of Molonga. The well-trained cadets rearranged themselves in a line and in a very organized manner, started to walk past the check post where one of Mr. Joi's team members checked the cadets before letting them through. Shijo leaned towards Sara, who was right behind him, and Kadis, who was bringing up the rear, and whispered with glee, 'This is going to be a cakewalk!'

No sooner had he said that, than a new officer appeared at the check post. Mr. Joi's face went pale and he whispered, 'Uh oh! The officer who was supposed to come to the post somehow hasn't made it, you see. And now the General himself is here for an inspection. His name is General Seiya and he wasn't scheduled to visit today. You see, I haven't been able to get a lot of information about the General. I need to work on that!'

General Seiya was a grumpy looking man with an air of superiority; his waxed, upturned moustache added to his stern look. He wore his uniform with great pride and strutted on his tall horse with his chest puffed up as he looked down on everyone.

Mr. Joi couldn't believe his bad luck – on the very day he was trying to smuggle in three youths from the enemy Kingdom, the highest ranked army officer should show up unscheduled. Seeing the look of alarm on Mr. Joi's face, the colour drained from the faces of the three young friends.

'So, what do we do now? Can we make a run for it and escape? Please say something!' cried the young Prince, nervously.

His right leg had started to shake as it always did when he was agitated and anxious. Mr. Joi shook his head, 'You see, it's too late to run. We'll be spotted. Just try to keep calm and carry on!'

'Easier said than done ...' whispered Sara.

Shijo joined in, 'As long as it's not easier dead than done ...'

Kadis gave Shijo a dirty look. 'Now is not the time for your silly jokes!'

As they got closer to the border post, Mr. Joi and his team member gave each other a quick look. The team member understood and started discussing something with the General to distract him. The other team member, taking his cue, missed counting a few cadets when the General was distracted. 'That was close,' thought Kadis. General Seiya looked at the remaining cadets as the count went on.

'98 ... 99 ... 100! All in sir!'

The three friends, prodded on discreetly by Mr. Joi, scurried in. They were now in Molongan territory. Suddenly, there was a loud shout. 'HALT!!'

With their hearts in their mouths, they turned to see that the General had dismounted his horse and was walking towards them. With an air of authority and self-importance, he walked up and stood in front of them imposingly. Mr. Joi tried to intervene but the General raised his hand, gesturing for him to stop. A few moments of intense silence followed, during which even the wind that was gently blowing stopped, as if afraid of him. Young Kadis' right leg started shaking again and he hoped the General wouldn't notice.

After glaring at the three friends for a few moments, the General looked them up and down and then started to circle them with slow, measured steps. Kadis held on tightly to the sack that housed the legendary sword. The General stopped right in front

of Kadis, whose leg was now quite out of control. In a gruff voice, he shouted, 'I understand all you cadets were on a hike ... but what is the matter with you three! LOOK AT YOUR UNIFORMS! IS THIS WHAT A FUTURE SOLDIER OF MOLONGA IS SUPPOSED TO LOOK LIKE?? WHY ARE YOUR UNIFORMS SO DIRTY??!!'

So he hadn't noticed that they were not part of the 100 cadets! The three friends and Mr. Joi couldn't have been more relieved. Mr. Joi scampered to the General's side, 'Sir, my apologies! Keeping them disciplined was my responsibility. It shall not happen again.'

The General looked sternly at Mr. Joi and said nothing for a few moments. Then he abruptly walked away. All four of them heaved a collective sigh of relief.

As they walked ahead, the other team members were rounding up the cadets and one of them gestured to Mr. Joi that it was now safe for them to discreetly exit and head to the safe house. Mr. Joi quickly bundled them up into a waiting carriage, mounted his horse and galloped to the front, leading the carriage towards the safe house. And it was only once they found themselves safely inside the carriage, relieved at having escaped so narrowly, that it hit them.

They were now inside the enemy territory of Molonga.

As they made their way to the safe house, Kadis slowly lifted the sword out of the sack and unwrapped the old grey-brown cloth that it was in. A faint glow emitted from the tip of the blade and one of the jewels on the handle flickered and glowed just a little.

Kadis peeked outside the window of the carriage. They were passing through small villages and wooded areas. The Kingdom of Molonga didn't look all that different from Kofu. The people, the land and the culture were almost identical. Then why couldn't their people live peacefully? Why couldn't war be abolished completely?

Late that afternoon, they arrived at the old stone cottage which was to be their safe house for the next few days. The cottage was in the middle of nowhere, at the foot of some mountains and was covered on all sides by tall trees and bushes.

The exhausted friends fell asleep as soon as they reached their rooms. It was dark by the time they woke up. As they walked out of their rooms, a surprise awaited them.

'Shonin!' cried Kadis excitedly as he ran to give him a hug along with Shijo and Sara. How the wise, old and mysterious Shonin had gotten there, and ahead of them at that, was a mystery to the trio. Shonin chuckled, 'Well, stop wondering! I do have my secret ways ... ways which are too dangerous to take you along on, hence the comparatively safer way of getting you in with the help of my friend Mr. Joi. He's now also helping me prepare some hot soup for the three of you.'

Mr. Joi proceeded to serve it to them and as they ate, Shonin continued, 'If I'm seen by the authorities here, they'll arrest me straight away as they'll assume I am here for some nefarious purpose.'

'Politics is indeed complicated,' thought Kadis. Mr. Joi explained, 'So you see, if the respected Shonin was found wandering around, it would give them great pleasure to arrest a member of the Kofu royal family.'

Shonin nodded, 'All the more reason to stop all this cloak-and-dagger business and get back to friendly and familial relations again, as they once were many years ago.'

'But all this hatred and enmity ... and war ... why does it start in the first place?' asked Sara.

Shonin took a deep breath. 'All wars in history have started due to false pride, greed or even the stupidity of some people. Whatever the reasons might be, mankind is not good at recognizing or admitting them, hence one side thinks they are more right than the other and war begins. It doesn't lead to anything but destruction and pain ...'

'... and that's why it has to be stopped,' added Sara enthusiastically.

Shonin smiled warmly, 'Exactly! And that's why you three brave soldiers of peace are here and have made it this far. "Well begun is half done", I always say and today is a great beginning. Get some rest and we'll speak more tomorrow, assuming I'm still here in this safe house and haven't had to secretly escape back to my home!'

The three friends managed to laugh at Shonin's words but secretly hoped he would still be there when they woke up.

❦ 20 ❧

The next morning, Shonin was gone. When they awoke, Mr. Joi greeted them with some warm tea and breakfast. He had no idea when or if Shonin would return. All he knew was that they had to plan the next course of action. The first step being to befriend Tara, the Princess of Molonga, Kadis' second cousin. Unlike the rest of her family who wanted to live in a grandiose manner and hold on to their royal status, she liked to move about freely among the common folk, much to the chagrin of her family. She hated conflict and believed that the state's resources could be put to better use than preparing for or going to war. Perhaps getting in touch with her secretly and working with her would bring about some positive result.

'What if we reveal ourselves as citizens of Kofu, of course connected to the royal family, and she hears us out but disagrees? Whatever her ideology may be, what if her loyalties to her family prevent her from siding with us or teaming with us? And also, what if she exposes us to the authorities as spies?' asked Kadis nervously.

Mr. Joi thought for a while in silence. He then stood up and looked at the three friends. 'You see, that's more reason for us to succeed. Failure, you see, is not an option!'

Kadis shook his head.

'Easier said than done ...'

Shijo rejoined, 'Easier dead than done!'

Kadis gave him a dirty look, 'Now don't you start that again.'

They all laughed nervously. Mr. Joi brought them back to reality.

'Step one, you see, is to befriend Tara. Not the worst mission in the world for a good-natured young Prince. Even though she is the enemy Princess, you see, she is your family after all.'

Kadis thought to himself, '*Family* that would like to see my father and me finished! Some family indeed.'

Shijo was quite intrigued on hearing about Princess Tara and her friendship with the common folk. 'So, this Princess Tara ... you say she likes being friends with commoners? And ... is she ... er, beautiful ...?'

Kadis and Sara understood what he was getting at.

'You see, once you meet her, I'm sure you will be struck by her beauty ... But before you get any ideas, the two Kingdoms would have to become friends again! How's that for some additional motivation?' Mr. Joi winked.

He then left them to eat and rest and promised to be back soon.

As soon as he left, Sara noticed that the sword had begun to glow a bit more.

'It really is true, the braver we become and the closer to our goal we get, the sooner the sword will return to its old glory ...' Sara said with a smile.

It was a couple of hours before Mr. Joi returned to the cottage. The three friends were waiting eagerly for some news. Mr. Joi took off his coat and smiled. 'I've dug up some useful information, you see. Tomorrow is farmer's market day in the neighbouring village and Tara will be there to support some of her friends at the market. That's where we should be. One of my team members has a daughter named Myo who is a good friend and aide of Tara, you see, and she will introduce you to the Princess. Tara will be told that you three live in a village at the far end of Molonga, a place she hasn't ever visited. So you see, it's all settled then. One step closer tomorrow!'

Mr. Joi started to leave, but then turned back suddenly to add, 'You see, because the village market is far away from the capital and near the border, most people carry swords or knives with them. It's not as safe as Kofu, especially if your cover is blown. You must carry the sword with you. It might actually need to be used for the purpose it was made ...'

ᴄᴈ 21 ᴈᴀ

The hustle and bustle of the village market was the first thing that struck the three friends as they walked through it. There were traders vociferously trying to sell their wares, citizens haggling over the rates and a constant buzz of voices and sounds. The clothes worn by the common folk were as bright and colourful as the market itself. The lanes were narrow and busy. It was lively, crowded and humming with activity.

The village market felt vaguely familiar to Kadis. Then he realized that while the topography of the area might be different, the ambience and culture were like Kofu's. Kadis was afraid of attracting attention. He gripped the old canvas bag tighter. Just as they were about to step forward, they were stopped by a young man.

'Are you young folk looking for anything in particular at the market?'

Kadis was startled by the sudden appearance of a stranger.

'Are you new around these parts?'

Kadis replied nervously, 'Well, um ... er ... kind of ...' when Sara discreetly kicked him on the shin.

They weren't supposed to let anyone know that they were new around here.

'In that case, please allow me to lead you to my stall here at the market ... the silks are exquisite, but not expensive!'

Before Sara and Shijo could stop him, the stranger took Kadis by the hand and almost forcefully led him towards his stall. On reaching there, Sara whispered in Kadis' ear, 'Let's just move on before we get into any trouble. We were supposed to meet Mr. Joi's contact, remember?'

Kadis was about to announce to the young stall keeper that he had to leave when two of the stall keeper's companions cornered him.

'Oh please, sir, just have a look at these silks, you look like a wealthy traveller with great taste!'

On seeing his discomfort, Sara and Shijo decided to act before things got out of hand. No sooner had they moved towards Kadis to rescue him, than the stall keeper adroitly stepped aside and snatched the old canvas bag that was in Kadis' hand: the bag that contained the sword.

In the few seconds it took the three friends to realize what had just happened, the thieving stall keeper dashed away from them at top speed.

'Stop! Thief!!' Kadis yelled out as the three friends began to give chase. This wasn't the first time the stall keeper and his companions had attempted a stunt such as this. They were notorious for stealing and pickpocketing, their targets being the traders who visited the market, often from faraway lands.

Sara, being the fastest of the three, was almost at his heels in just under a minute but the thief was not one to be outsmarted so easily. He threw the bag towards his companion who then ran off down another alley. The three friends changed direction and now began to run after the companion instead. A thrilling chase ensued with the thief getting the better of the friends as he knew the alleyways like the back of his hand. Once again Sara got close enough to catch him but he suddenly took hold of a pole that stood supporting the awning of a store and leapt upwards onto the roof of the store, scaling the wall beyond.

The thief was gone. He was now on the other side, in the next alleyway. Kadis had almost resigned himself to his fate when Sara, seething with rage, pulled herself up on the awning and scaled the top of the wall. Shijo followed suit. Kadis was forced to follow or he risked losing sight of his friends here in enemy territory. His fear of being separated from his friends, enabled him to not only jump onto the awning but also scale the wall beyond. As he landed, he saw the thief running hard with Sara and Shijo in hot pursuit. Kadis ran behind them as fast as he could. Suddenly, as the thief made a sharp turn, a stone shot out of nowhere and hit him directly on his right ear and the next instant he slammed onto the ground. The three friends came to a screeching halt.

The thief had been knocked out of his senses by the stone.

22

'There's your thief!'

The three friends turned to see a beautiful young girl, dressed casually in simple, colourful clothes, carrying herself in a way that betrayed her wealth and nobility. She had a slingshot in her hand which was the weapon that had brought the thief down. As she stopped by the unconscious lad on the ground, she said to the friends, 'I've been wanting to catch this gang for a while now. Thanks to his thievery today, I've got him.'

Before the three friends could understand what was happening, another attractive-looking young girl of similar age walked into the alley along with a uniformed guard. They were followed by an older man with well-groomed salt-and-pepper hair and beard. He had a dignified air about him and wore black robes with the royal crest on his tunic. The girl with the slingshot gestured to the uniformed guard who promptly picked up the thief. 'Have him arrested. And make sure he tells you about his two companions. I will have no more of this gang of thieves harassing the traders in this border town.'

The uniformed guard bowed respectfully. 'Yes, Your Highness.' He then quietly withdrew with his prisoner.

The regal-looking young girl bent over, picked up the old and tattered canvas bag and handed it to Kadis with a smile, saying, 'Your

almost-stolen bag!'

'So this is my cousin, the Princess,' thought Kadis to himself.

Then her friend spoke up, 'Um, hello, if I'm not mistaken, aren't you the guests of my uncle Mr. Joi who works with the border corps?'

While Shijo and Kadis were a bit taken aback, Sara soon realized that this was none other than the Princess' friend who was to meet them at the market and introduce them to Princess Tara.

'Yes ... Yes, we are!'

She then discreetly nodded to the two boys. Kadis understood.

'Uh ... we were on our way to meet you when our bag got stolen,' he explained.

'I'm Myo.' She held out her hand, introducing herself.

'Kadis', 'Sara', 'Shijo'. The three friends introduced themselves and then turned to the Princess, who held out her hand in a casual friendly way.

'Tara.'

'Not just Tara, but Princess Tara, my childhood friend,' Myo said proudly.

Tara, looking visibly embarrassed, quickly added, 'Just Tara will do!'

She then gestured towards the older man in the gathering. 'This here is my most trusted guard whom I affectionately call Binko. He has looked after me since I was six. After my father, it's him I trust the most.'

Binko nodded his head in acknowledgement.

Then turning to the Princess, Kadis said, 'We cannot thank you enough for saving our bag. You have no idea how important that bag is for all of us!'

'What's in the bag?' asked Tara.

Before Kadis could come up with a suitable reply, Sara interjected, 'Oh just our basic belongings, nothing fancy.'

'You didn't tell me you had to meet some friends at the market,' Tara said to Myo.

'Actually ...' Before Myo could complete what she was saying, Tara threw another question at her, 'And where are your friends from? They're not dressed very Molongan!' she observed with a smile.

Seeing the nervous look on the faces of the three friends, Myo quickly explained, 'The thing is, these three live in the village of Nikato, just by the foot of the mountains. This is the first time they've travelled so far from home to the other end of Molonga.'

'Nikato? Hmmm, I've only visited Nikato once, many years ago when I was a little girl ... haven't visited since. I guess because nothing much happens there. I remember it to be a peaceful little village at the foot of the hills. It's these border villages where we are now that I'm concerned about. They need to be cleaned up and made more secure.'

'That's er ... correct ... I guess ...' Myo replied.

Kadis wanted to keep up the friendly conversation and looked at Shijo, but Shijo seemed to have no interest whatsoever in the conversation. He was staring at Myo and seemed quite smitten by her!

Relieved that the introductions had gone smoothly, Myo said,

'Er, Tara ... I was to spend the weekend with these friends. Is it alright if they walk around with us? That way I can be with you and them all at once ...'

The Princess took another discreet look at the three newcomers. Their awkwardness was actually quite appealing. She smiled at Myo, 'Of course, you can show them around. They're welcome to tag along with us.'

As she and Myo turned to walk on, Kadis looked at his friends with a sigh of relief and clutched his tattered old bag tightly as they walked behind the two young girls. Tara's loyal guard Binko followed at a short distance. Though he was a lot older, he looked tough enough to take on twenty. Kadis hoped he'd never get on his wrong side. He was trying hard to figure out how he could broach the topic of peace between the two Kingdoms. Shijo, on his part, was rather busy too. Busy focusing his attention on Myo. Though Myo didn't let on, she quite enjoyed the attention she was receiving from the shy boy.

Princess Tara continued her morning round of the farmer's market. 'I like to see how the local folk are doing and love these markets as all the citizens are out and about enjoying both the atmosphere and the good weather. However, I do wish these villages at the border were safer than they presently are,' Tara explained.

Kadis was relieved that back home in Kofu, they didn't have any such safety issues. If Molonga was united with Kofu once again, he would make sure he spoke to his father about the safety issues in these villages.

At lunchtime Tara made a suggestion that sent a shiver down

the spines of Kadis, Shijo and Sara.

'I have an idea. How about we pop over to the nearby army camp to lunch with my uncle, General Seiya. He's my mother's brother. Though I'm his niece, he loves me like he would his own child.'

General Seiya!

Kadis felt as if a ton of bricks had fallen on his head. Of all the people, her uncle had to be the very same army General who had inspected them at the border. He blurted out, 'Er ... I think we should stick around here at the market ... it's so nice here ... don't you think?'

He gave Shijo a hard nudge, but Shijo was so mesmerized by Myo he hadn't paid attention to who Tara's uncle was.

'I'm quite happy to go for lunch with our hosts for the day, wherever they would like us to go. Seems a better option than the market for sure ... right, Myo?'

Myo smiled in reply. Kadis tried to protest, 'B-but we should be at the market ...'

Before Sara could say anything, Tara exclaimed, 'Nonsense! You three please join me at my uncle's for lunch. I will not take no for an answer. Any friends of Myo are friends of mine.'

The matter was settled. The Princess had spoken. They were to lunch in the lion's den. As Binko walked on ahead to arrange the carriages, Sara gave Shijo a kick in the shin as discreetly as she could.

'ow!' screamed out Shijo.

'What happened?' asked Myo quickly.

Before Shijo could reply, Sara said, 'Oh nothing, just a bug that bit our poor Shijo!'

Well, our poor Shijo didn't quite understand what was going on and it was only when Tara and Myo turned their attention to the arriving carriages that Sara whispered in his ear, 'You imbecile! Tara's uncle is none other than the same sour-faced army General who inspected us at the border. Start paying attention!'

The two frightened boys followed a fuming Sara into the carriage that was to travel behind the one that carried Tara and Myo. To add to their woes, there was an armed guard near the driver at the front of each carriage and Binko led the way on horseback in front of the Princess' carriage. Once they were at the army cantonment they would be surrounded by enemy guards and soldiers. They had quite literally gone from the frying pan into the fire.

23

'TEN-SHUN!'
General Seiya's thunderous voice shook the room. Not known for social graces, this is how he greeted his guests, just as he would order his troops before inspection. He slowly circled Princess Tara's three young guests, inspecting them up and down. His impeccably waxed and upturned moustache added to his aura. The three friends could hardly breathe. When General Seiya had seen them at the border, their faces were covered in mud. So, much to their relief, he didn't recognize them now. Tara and Myo couldn't help giggling at their obvious discomfort.

'A bit sloppy, if you ask me, but what else can one expect from the younger generation. A stint in the army will set you three slobs straight!' barked the General as he completed his inspection of his guests.

'AT EASE!' He ordered them gruffly before settling into a large chair and lighting his pipe. Tara said, 'It's alright now. That means you can relax and have a seat.'

It took a moment for the friends to gather their wits. Kadis was still shaking with fear as a Corporal offered the three some fresh juice.

'So, Nikato eh?' The gruff voice of the General rolled out of his mouth like thunder on a stormy night. 'And what family in Nikato do you belong to?'

Kadis' mouth went dry. Now what name could he make up that would sound authentic? They were surely going to get caught. Myo quickly came to his rescue, 'Uh ... General ... they're the children of Mikko, the apple orchard owner ...'

'Hmmph! I could have sworn that old Mikko had only two children. Anyway, be that as it may, I will send word to him that he should discipline his children more strictly. You three here are quite sloppy in your demeanour! As I was suggesting, you all should join the army for training ...'

Before he could continue, Tara interrupted, 'Er uncle, what's for lunch today?'

'Hmmph!'

General Seiya hated being interrupted when he was trying to influence the younger generation to join the army.

'No junk food today, if that's what you're asking. It's a healthy menu and you all better finish what's on your plates.'

Kadis was so afraid of the General that he would have eaten a live frog had he been ordered to.

The luncheon followed for the most part in complete silence which suited Kadis and his friends perfectly. Across the big table, Tara and Myo seemed to be enjoying the uneasiness of their new friends a lot more than what was on their plates.

When dessert was served, General Seiya refused to eat any. 'Hmmph! The days of dessert are over. I have to watch what I eat so I can be battle ready. Those Kofu-ites need to be shown who

is boss, after all!'

Kadis almost choked on his dessert on hearing these words. Now that the subject had been broached, Sara—being the brave one—decided to bell the cat.

'Er ... ahem ... General Seiya ... is there going to be war soon? Is there anything we need to be concerned about ... I mean as citizens of er ... M-Molonga I mean ...'

There was silence in the room. Kadis couldn't believe that Sara would actually speak up in front of the General, let alone ask about his battle plans.

General Seiya looked up from his plate and the tension in the air could be cut with a knife.

'Concerned? Do you need to be *concerned*?? HMMPH!! That is none of your concern, young lady!'

After a moment's pause, the General added, 'The enemy are the ones who need to be concerned. Not you citizens of Molonga.'

Sara, though somewhat nervous now, asked bravely, 'Er ... Sir ... General ... by enemy you mean ... K-Kofu, right?'

General Seiya looked at her and a moment later the right side of his mouth curved into a half-smile. 'There won't be an enemy soon enough ... not after they are taught a lesson and flattened to the ground!' he said proudly.

This wasn't good news for the three friends. Encouraged by Sara's questions, Shijo asked one of his own, 'Er, Mister General ... I mean Sir ... wh-when is this aforementioned f-flattening going to take place?'

The half-smile that had formed on the General's mouth

instantly vanished. 'And why do you ask, young man? Are you keen to join me in battle? Are you? You're lucky you're a friend of the Princess!'

Shijo regretted his question more than he had ever regretted anything in life. Before he could attempt a reply, the Corporal walked up to the General and whispered something in his year.

'HMPPH! I thought I said after lunch! Anyway, seat him in the war room and I'll be there shortly.'

The Corporal swiftly left. General Seiya wiped his mouth, had a sip of water, then pushing his chair back forcefully, he excused himself from the dining area.

Princess Tara looked at the young friends and couldn't help giggling at their expressions. Myo too started to chuckle. Kadis finally spoke up, 'Excuse me ... Princess Tara ... now that lunch is done, why don't you show us around a bit before we head back ... We're so excited to be here at the army headquarters!'

Sara and Shijo couldn't believe that Kadis had gathered the nerve to ask the Princess this question, let alone any question. Sara then gestured to them to look down towards the sack that young Kadis had brought along. It lay on the floor between them but was emitting a very faint glow, noticeable only to them as the sack was not visible to anyone else. Kadis' brave question had made the sword glow.

24

Tara first showed the trio around the palatial house and then led them out into the grounds.

'I think we should try and find out what the General here is planning. I've done my bit, now it's up to you both,' whispered Kadis to his friends when Tara was out of earshot.

Soon the army headquarters came into view. As they walked by an open window they heard the familiar gruff voice of the General. Kadis, Sara and Shijo stopped to listen while Tara and Myo continued walking ahead. The General seemed to be having a heated discussion with a junior officer.

'HMMPH! So, you had some minor changes to suggest, eh, Major? I think not! These plans work for me just as they are!'

He then haughtily shut the file and left the room. The Major and the Corporal meekly followed General Seiya to pacify him. The file was now lying on the table unattended. 'This is our chance to find out their plans,' Sara whispered.

'A golden opportunity indeed but a risky one too!' whispered Kadis, nervously.

Shijo, however, agreed with Sara. 'She's right. All one of us has to do is step through those windows, have a quick glance at the contents of that report, memorize them accurately and report back here. A matter of five minutes, tops!'

Tara and Myo backtracked to see what was holding back the trio. When Myo spotted them in deep discussion outside the General's office window she realized they were up to something. Kadis, Sara and Shijo noticed Tara looking at them questioningly. Shijo quickly blurted out, 'Oh, Kadis here is feeling exhausted. He wants to just sit here in the shade while we are shown around by you and Tara ... er I mean *Princess* Tara ...!'

Kadis had no intention of being left here all alone to undertake this crazy mission by himself.

Tara nodded, 'Oh, but I thought you were most keen to look around the army camp.'

Kadis replied weakly, 'Er, yes but so are my friends here. I m-mean they are probably even keener than I am ...'

Even though she didn't seem convinced, Tara shrugged, 'That's fine, we'll be back in half an hour to pick you up. And if you feel like resting, you could walk back to my uncle's house and lie down for a bit.'

'B-but ... maybe I can come with you all ... actually er ... um ...' stuttered Kadis but Tara gently gestured for him to sit under the shady tree.

Kadis gave Shijo a stern look for the mess he had gotten him into.

Kadis was now all alone. He saw the General and his two companions walking across the grounds towards a small building in the distance. He looked back into the room. It was still empty. His leg started shaking as it always did when he was nervous. Kadis held on to the sack tightly to help comfort himself. He then gingerly heaved himself over the threshold of the window and toppled into the room. After he had caught his breath, Kadis looked around. There was the dastardly file right in front of him. With a shaking hand, he slid the file closer to him and started reading, looking up every couple of seconds to check if anyone was walking by. As he read on his nervousness gave way to concentration. He turned the pages and read on for some time, lost in the information he was being made privy to.

Just as he was on the last page, he heard footsteps outside the door and the familiar gruff 'HMMPH!'

Kadis froze! In a moment of complete panic, he tried to jump behind the couch to take cover, but landed with a thud on the couch instead. As Kadis lay there stunned at his own lack of athletic skills, the door opened and the General walked in, followed by the Major and the Corporal. They stopped dead in their tracks on seeing the young lad lying on the couch. Not knowing what to do Kadis lay there and shut his eyes, almost waiting for an execution order. 'This is it,' he thought to himself, 'the last day of my life.' He lay there in wait for a few seconds and when nothing happened, he opened his eyes to see the General standing right next to him.

'And *what*, may I ask, are you doing here, without my permission? And where is Tara? Why aren't you with her and your other sloppy friends? What is the meaning of this?!'

'Uh ... er ... .um ...' was the best reply Kadis could come up with.

'HMMPH!' grunted General Seiya when a voice, almost angelic in its tone, saved the day for Kadis.

'Oh, uncle, you do remember Kadis, he was at lunch with me. We were out for a walk in the grounds when he started to feel ill so we asked him to lie down. He must have entered the office to stay in the shade and lay down on the couch.'

The General stepped back a bit. Kadis immediately got up and stood to attention. 'HMMPH!' Civilian kids! NO character! True character is only found in the soldiers of the army. A little sun and some wholesome, nutritious food and you find yourself all exhausted and laid up. Terribly weak constitution, I say! I must have a word with Mikko about his boy. You need to join the army and toughen up, young lad!'

'Er sorry, sir ... I alopogize ... I agopolize ... I apogolize ...'

'I think he wishes to *apologize,*' interrupted Tara.

'I get the idea. HMMPH!! You may leave now!'

Before he could finish his sentence, Kadis had bolted out of the room. The rest followed.

They regrouped and started to walk away when the familiar gruff voice halted them in their tracks, 'BOY! YOU THERE!'

The trio stopped and slowly turned, expecting the worst. General Seiya was standing by the window with his hands on his hips.

'Don't forget to take your dirty sack with you!'

Kadis clumsily climbed through the window, pounced on the sack and jumped back outside to where his friends were. General Seiya turned back to his officers muttering,

'Civilians! No character ... HMMPH!'

❧ 25 ❧

As they all walked back to the royal carriages, Tara turned to Kadis who was still shaking from his encounter with the General.

'Take care of your health, Kadis. Where will you three be staying on your visit here?' 'With me!' said Myo, words which brought a wide smile to Shijo's face.

'In that case, feel free to join me tomorrow as well. Myo stays within the castle grounds so I'll see you all soon. Myo, you can take them to your home in the other carriage. I'll go back in this one.'

As they were getting into the second carriage Kadis gave Shijo a dirty look. 'A fine mess you got me into!'

Before Shijo could reply, Sara said, 'A fine mess he *almost* got you into! So, did you ...?'

Kadis nodded in the affirmative. Shijo and Sara jumped in glee and gave Kadis a tight hug. As they got into the carriage, Kadis promised to tell them everything once they were in the safe confines of Myo's home. A faint glow fell on his face as he spoke. Sara and Shijo smiled as they knew where it came from.

It was a full moon night, and the castle grounds were awash with moonlight. At the far end of the castle grounds was a row of small houses for the staff working directly with the royal family. Amongst them, Myo's quarters were the closest to the castle building. The three friends sat by the fireplace with Myo. Kadis was giving Shijo a piece of his mind. 'I did the groundwork and expected you or Sara to go ahead and read the General's secret file. But you both ran off and left me there all by myself!'

Shijo looked suitably sheepish in return, knowing that anything he said might reveal his feelings for Myo.

Sara, being the voice of reason, steered the conversation back on course. 'So shall we please get back to the matter at hand? Kadis, what information could you gather from those secret papers?'

Kadis took a deep breath to quell the butterflies in his stomach, 'So what I understood from the report is that the Molongans are definitely preparing a major attack on Kofu. They have a highly trained army that will carry out the attack at our southern border and a naval fleet that will attack by sea in the north. Both fronts at the same time ... and sooner than my father thinks. He expects no movement from them for at least a month and is preparing accordingly. But the Molongans are planning to attack in the next five days.'

This was far more serious than any of the listeners had expected. But they were in for another shock from Kadis. 'I'm not done, so please calm down and listen up. The worst is yet to come. Due to some secret surveillance and reconnaissance by their elite commando unit, they suspect there's a secret passage which can bypass the big wall into Kofu. They don't yet know where it is but are certain it's there somewhere!'

It was Sara's turn to be in shock. 'Secret passage? Oh, my gosh, OUR secret passage? The one that your granduncle Shonin showed

us that leads straight into Kofu?'

'Yes, I'm sure they mean the same one! How many secret passages can there be?'

There were a few minutes of stunned silence before Kadis spoke up again. 'And listen to this: their elite commando unit is planning to find that secret passage and a team of three is already exploring the area stealthily. Once they discover the secret passage, they will use it to get them in so they can create havoc from the inside in our army camp – just before the Molongan army and navy begin their simultaneous attack from outside the wall and from the seafronts. Basically, it will be a synchronized attack across three fronts!'

The friends were at a loss for words.

Suddenly, they heard a sniff. With a start, they all turned towards the door and were shocked to see Princess Tara standing there, her eyes red with rage and tears of disappointment flowing down her cheeks. She had heard the entire conversation.

❧ 26 ☙

T he friends were stunned to see Tara at the door. Tara stood there trying to take in the betrayal that was playing out in front of her. Her attendant and best friend Myo, along with two friends whom she vouched for, were using Tara to spy on Molonga. They were all from Kofu. They were the enemy!

Kadis and Shijo were dumbstruck. Time had slowed down and they didn't know what to do next. Sara, on the other hand, was quick to respond. She could see that Tara was just about to turn and leave the room, to lock it from the outside and alert the guards. But, before she could do so, Sara slammed the door shut, thus cutting off Tara's only exit.

'Get up and stop her from leaving! NOW!' she shouted to Shijo and Kadis.

It worked. Jolted out of their stunned state by the quick-witted Sara, they jumped up and sprang into action. Kadis flattened his back to the door to thwart any attempt by Tara to open it while Shijo held her hands from behind in a firm grip. After a brief struggle, the trio managed to gag her mouth with a piece of cloth, and forced her to sit on a chair with her hands tied behind it with a long scarf. Tara struggled to break free but soon gave up and only a faint muffled sound emerged from her mouth. Secure in the knowledge that Tara wasn't going anywhere for a while, Kadis broke the silence. 'I think we need to explain ourselves to the Princess.'

'Go ahead then,' Sara prodded.

'Me?!' asked Kadis.

'It's only fitting that a Prince speak to a Princess. Besides, she's your cousin after all.'

Tara realized with a shock that Kadis was the Prince of Kofu.

Kadis cleared his throat. 'Tara, as you've come to understand, my name is Kadis and I'm the Prince of Kofu. That makes me your cousin. And that makes us family. I would like to explain why we are here. We have risked everything, are unarmed and are in your Kingdom. It's only a matter of time before your guards come looking for you. And then we'll be done for. For us, there's no escape. You're the only one who can save the four of us. You're the only one who can save both Molonga and Kofu.'

Kadis mustered up the courage to continue, 'I know the story of how the once united Kingdoms separated. There's no point going into who was at fault. What's done is done. The fault always lies with both. Our granduncle Shonin told us how the Kingdoms and thus the families came to be estranged. We have to now look to the future and not the past.'

Kadis went up to the old tattered sack and slowly pulled out the sword. Tara's eyes widened in horror. This was the same sword that belonged to her side of the family. It was now a symbol of the animosity between the two Kingdoms. Kadis was going to kill her with that sword! She struggled to free herself as Kadis walked up to her with the sword in his hand. The sword glowed eerily, bathing the room in its hue. Tara shut her eyes, anticipating the worst. Instead, she once again heard the soothing voice of her cousin.

'I know the story of this sword. We stand here before you humbly as soldiers ...'

Tara looked on, not able to understand where this was going. Kadis smiled warmly, 'Soldiers not of war, but of peace.'

He knelt beside his cousin and gently started to untie her hands. Surprised, she didn't attempt to escape but felt compelled to hear him out.

'We know of the war, the attack being planned on Kofu. I've never fought in one but I can say with utmost assurance that war doesn't benefit anyone. Neither the victor, nor the vanquished. We were once family, but ego and stupidity have led us to this stage. We've humbly come here to return this very sword as a gesture of peace and put a stop to the years of hate and enmity between us.'

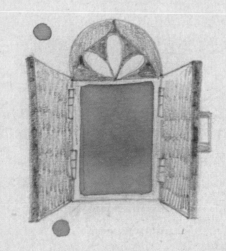

Kadis' eloquence had moved Tara and his own friends almost to tears. He continued, 'My family and my Kingdom are preparing for war too. We must stop this madness – together we can. You and I, we are the same. Our Kingdoms have similar problems, similar cultures, and people on both sides just want to live a happy life

peacefully. We've come to seek your help so that we, the Kingdoms of Molonga and Kofu … the people … you and I … can be family once again.'

There was silence in the room. A peaceful silence. As if a hush had descended in the middle of a storm. Tara slowly removed the gag from her mouth and saw the Prince of Kofu on his knees right in front of her. How could a boy so gentle mean any harm? How could a boy so aglow with compassion and courage be anything but a soldier of peace? She placed her hands on his shoulders and rose up with him. Looking into his eyes, she gave him a warm embrace. Nothing was said on either side, but the silence spoke volumes. In his heart, at that moment, Kadis knew that there was the distinct possibility of peace for both the Kingdoms.

******

Standing by the window, Kadis cupped the wings of the big falcon and raised his hands towards the sky. The bird flapped its large wings with graceful ease and flew away. Kadis had used the secret whistle to call for the falcon and had attached a scroll with an important message for Shonin.

'She has understood our mission and is now with us. I've read the General's plans. They plan to find our secret passage and use it to enter Kofu. Attack from inside and the two fronts. Not much time left. Please advise. Kadis.'

The young Prince watched the magnificent bird soar into the skies with their precious message. 'How far we have come,' he thought to himself. 'A few weeks ago, if I had been told I would be deep within enemy territory and be reconciled with my cousin, the enemy Princess, I would have baulked at the idea. Today it has actually happened. But it isn't a time to rejoice. Not just yet.'

'What next?' Kadis asked his friends. This was the question uppermost in all their minds. They knew there were no easy answers to that. Exhausted by all that they were going through, they fell into a deep sleep.

A loud banging on the door just before dawn woke them up with a start. Myo ran to the door. A loud voice shouted out from the other side. 'It is the Royal Guard! The Princess hasn't returned to her quarters. Open the door NOW!'

Everyone inside gasped; they had been so exhausted last night that they missed the fact that Princess Tara had to return to the castle. She now gestured to Myo to open the door. The two guards came rushing in followed by several others. There were more waiting outside.

'The Princess was last seen with you ...' the panic-stricken guard started to say, but he stopped when he saw the sleepy Princess looking hale and hearty.

On seeing the guards, Tara tried to calm them down. 'No need to panic! I was in the company of friends.'

Binko entered the room and hurriedly walked up to the Princess, bowing respectfully. Tara smiled warmly at him. Binko gave the group a cursory glance before turning back to the Princess. 'Your Highness, please come along with us without delay. Orders from His Highness King Toki himself.'

Tara turned to her friends and cousin. 'Guess it's time to go. But I'll see you all soon!' she exclaimed happily.

Just as Tara turned to leave, events took an unexpected turn.

The chief of the Royal Guard walked up sternly to Kadis and proclaimed, 'You are under arrest with immediate effect!'

The young Prince's face went pale. Tara started to rush towards her friends, but the chief of the guards held out his hand in a stern gesture to stop her. 'I'm sorry, Your Highness. We have express orders to take you to the King right away and to arrest all these young spies in the room,' he said while pointing towards Kadis, Sara, Shijo and Myo.

'But they're not spies ... they're my friends!' screamed Tara in protest, as two female guards began to escort her out.

'Apologies, Your Highness, but you're to be rescued from these spies for your own safety,' said Binko firmly.

The chief guard then turned to the terrified group of youngsters. As they were dragged away, the last thing Kadis remembered before passing out was the old sack which housed the sword, lying unseen under one of the beds.

******

When Kadis came to, he found himself in an unknown location. His head was throbbing with pain. It was dark and damp. The flickering light from a flaming torch filtered in from one direction, casting strange, eerie shadows on the rough stone walls. As his eyes slowly adjusted to his new surroundings, he realized he was in a dungeon of some sort, most likely within the walls of the castle itself. Spread out on the floor of the cell were Sara and Shijo who were still unconscious. In the far corner, Myo sat huddled. Kadis knelt beside her and tried to console her.

'I'm scared ...' said a distraught Myo in between sobs.

Kadis nodded, trying not to show how scared he himself was. Once Shijo and Sara were awake, Myo composed herself and spoke in hushed tones, 'As far as I can comprehend, we're in the dungeon which is below the main building of the castle complex. Tara lives with her parents high above this stone ceiling. This dungeon was built many years back to imprison people who were awaiting a sentence from the King. We have been branded as spies and that ... that is considered a very serious crime indeed,' she said with a trembling voice.

Sara wondered aloud, 'How did we ever get found out? I mean, Princess Tara had just found out herself last night and she understood our position.'

'Where is Shonin when we need him the most? I wish he were here to help us ...' said Kadis.

As if on cue, there was the heavy, creaking sound of an old door being pushed open somewhere above. Followed by the sound of footsteps on the cold, hard, stone floor and muffled voices that were fast approaching their cell. The next moment, they heard the sound of a key turning the lock to open the heavy door. The light from a flaming torch filled the room as four men entered. Even as the four tried to adjust their eyes to the light, they heard the now-familiar gruff voice, 'HMMPH!'

General Seiya was here himself to give them a welcome. 'I should have followed my instincts and never trusted this filthy little civilian spy!' the General said, looking directly at Kadis.

'Er, General, I was curious to know what kind of decision His Highness King Toki would make about these, er, prisoners, you see ...' one of the other men asked.

Joi! That had to be Mr. Joi! Mr. Joi stepped into the light. The young prisoners could have never imagined they would be so happy to see the rotund, jolly face of old Mr. Joi, or to hear his oft repeated 'you see'. They could see a faint smile of relief on Mr. Joi's face too.

'Decision? I would think a decision that would not go down very well with these spies!' The General stepped forward towards Kadis, the orange light from the flame flickering ominously on his face.

'So, you must have seen my reports when you feigned your illness in my office, eh? It never occurred to me that a weak and harmless looking fellow such as you would have it in him to be a spy.'

Just as he was leaning forward threateningly towards Kadis, Tara rushed into the dungeon, followed closely by Binko.

'General, I tried to stop her ...' Binko tried to explain but he was interrupted by General Seiya, 'HMMPH! But you were not good enough at your job to stop her, eh, Binko?'

But then he smiled, with a hint of pride, 'She is my niece after all. Strong-minded and fierce like her uncle.'

He held Tara by the shoulders. 'It troubles me to see my niece sympathize with the enemy. These cunning little foxes tried to send a message via falcon to someone in Kofu. We intercepted it and managed to get the scroll out of its claws. But the dirty bird somehow got away. What's more important than that silly bird, however, is this devious message we found. Joi, go ahead and read out that message!' he roared.

A nervous Mr. Joi took the scroll out of the messenger bag that was slung across his torso. He cleared his throat and began to read. 'She has understood our mission and is now with us. And I read the General's plans. They plan to find our secret passage and use it to enter Kofu. Attack from inside and the two fronts. Not much time left. Please advise. Kadis.'

'HMMPH! So you see, my dear Tara? The "she" they were referring to must be your companion Myo. They obviously brainwashed the poor girl. She had joined them in their dastardly mission. I'm sad to say that she's now one of them and will be branded a traitor by your father.'

So saying, he haughtily started to walk out of the cell followed by the other officers. Tara, sobbing sadly, was the last to leave. Suddenly Mr. Joi came running back and shouted at the young prisoners accusingly, 'WHAT?! What did you just say?'

He then turned to the General, 'Sir, I need to teach these insolent kids a lesson, you see, just like I teach my cadets when they step out of line. With your permission, sir!'

General Seiya turned to look at an angry looking Mr. Joi.

'HMMPH!' he said gruffly and stormed out of the cell.

❦ 28 ❧

Once everyone had left, Mr. Joi kneeled in front of the frightened group of kids.

'Please try and listen to me, you see. I understand what you're going through. But now is not the time to give up. When things are at their worst, that is the time to have stronger faith and be even more positive. That is the only thing you can do, you see.'

Shijo looked up teary-eyed at Mr. Joi, 'Easier said than done!'

Mr. Joi put his hand on Shijo's shoulder and said, 'I've been in touch with Shonin. The good thing is that the King thinks the "she" that you wrote of in the scroll is Myo. So Princess Tara is off the hook and now being on our side will still try to help. Secondly, Shonin has devised a plan to get you all out of here. Once out ...'

Before he could compete the sentence, Kadis interrupted him, 'Once out, we have to first retrieve the sword. It is presently lying under the bed in Myo's home.'

Mr. Joi thought for a moment, then spoke up. 'Yes – retrieving the sword is very important. Once we get you out of here, we head to Myo's quarters. We retrieve the sword, you see, then I smuggle you to the safe house where we had first kept you hidden. Once we are there, you see, Shonin will send word of what we could do next. That's all I have for now.'

'It's not going to be easy ...' Shijo sounded frightened.

And for the first time, Kadis sounded braver than the others. 'It sure will be easier than rotting in this damp, dark cell waiting to be taken to the gallows. Now *that* I'm really scared of!'

'Kadis is right,' agreed Sara.

'So, when will the plan come into effect?' asked Kadis.

There was silence for a few moments and then Mr. Joi replied, 'Now.'

'Now?' asked Kadis.

Mr. Joi nodded, 'There's no choice. One of my spies works here, you see. We stationed one person here just in case any of us was imprisoned. He'll leave your door open and divert the two guards on duty above the stairs. That's when you'll make your escape. I'll meet you just outside the caged door at the end of the long narrow passage that leads to the rear grounds of the castle. Once we regroup there, you see, we can proceed to the safe house. And then I report to HQ as if nothing happened. Good luck, kids! I have to leave. I'll lock the door and once I go up, I'll hand over the key and my colleague will be down shortly. Be safe, you see, and remember, time is of the essence!'

Soon after saying this, Mr. Joi hurried out.

'But ... but ...' Kadis tried to call out to him, but Mr. Joi locked the door and was heard making his way up the stone staircase. They were enveloped in darkness again.

'What's going to happen to us? We are done for ...' Myo started to sob.

'SHHH!' said Kadis, urgently.

Everyone looked at Kadis. Something had come over him in the last few moments. Where there was once anxiety and nervousness written all over his face, now there was only steely determination. 'Let's do this. Let's get out of here alive, put a stop to this war and get back home!'

Sara smiled, 'If you insist!'

A few moments later they heard footsteps approach. The heavy door was pulled open and a stern looking guard walked in with four bowls of porridge. This must be the guard that Mr. Joi had told them about. The four friends braced themselves for their escape. Myo even tried to smile at the guard, who ignored her and walked away. Much to their chagrin, the guard slammed the cell door shut, turned the key and locked them in again. Whatever happened to

Mr. Joi's plan? Just then they heard another set of footsteps running down hurriedly. The key turned and the heavy door was once again laboriously opened. A different guard entered this time, carrying a jug of water. As he walked in, he nodded to Kadis and the rest and whispered, 'Mr. Joi sent me.'

He then shouted in a loud voice, so that the guards upstairs might hear, 'Finish that porridge or else you won't get anything else to eat. And here's your water, you filthy scoundrels!'

He bowed respectfully to Prince Kadis and whispered, 'Sorry for the harsh words, my Prince. After a short wait please come out of the cell and make your way up the stairs. I'll distract the other two guards and show you the way to the passage. May good fortune shine on you.'

The guard then turned and left, slamming the door shut with a loud bang. A few moments later the door slowly creaked open just a crack. As promised, the kind guard had left the door slightly ajar.

The next few minutes seemed like hours. Finally, Kadis turned to his friends. They saw in his eyes a determination to succeed that they had never seen before. He stood up and walked to the door. The others took a deep breath and followed. Kadis peeked through the opening, then pushed the door open ever so slightly. The door let out a loud creak. He stopped to listen. Nothing. A bead of sweat formed on his brow as he pushed the door open just enough for one person to pass. Leading the way, he slid through and took a deep breath of relief when he realized there was no one else outside the heavy door. The others followed slowly behind him until they were all free of the dark cell.

They were in a small stone chamber lit by a lone torch on the wall. Theirs was the only cell in that chamber. Towards the far right was the first step of a staircase. Kadis slowly walked up to it and looked up. It was completely dark. They would have to venture up the stairs to see what lay beyond. Step by unsure step, Kadis began to climb up, followed closely by Sara, Myo and Shijo. It was a narrow stairway with just enough room for one person to walk through. A claustrophobe's nightmare. It was an immense struggle for the young Prince to not let the narrow walls close in on him. He ploughed on, feeling his way through the darkness till he saw a faint patch of light with some shadows flickering on the stone wall further up.

As the four friends reached the summit, their hearts pounded loudly in their chests. The glow from the torch outside was bright enough to show the way. Kadis leaned over to check if there was anyone outside. It seemed safe so he took a step forward towards the torch. Just as he was about to take another, there was a loud shout.

'YOU THERE!'

The loud voice caused their hearts to leap out of their mouths. They stopped and leaned back into the shadows. Then they heard another voice. The kind guard who had helped them called out, 'What? Why do you have to scream? I can hear you!'

The first voice spoke up again, even louder than before, 'Where are you off to? You're leaving your post.'

'I'm not leaving my post; I'm going by the small window on the far side to smoke my pipe,' Mr. Joi's friend answered.

'What about the prisoners?'

'Oh, they're not going anywhere!' he added, quickly.

They heard footsteps walking away. And then the voice of a third guard. 'You know, a pipe sounds like a good idea right now. You're right, we'll still be at our posts, just standing there a short distance away by the window. And those spies are just kids who are terribly scared. They won't try anything funny. I'm coming to the window too.'

A moment later, the first voice spoke up, 'Fine! No point me standing here by myself while you fools enjoy your pipe.'

And they heard him follow the other two.

As Kadis and his friends stepped out of the shadows they found themselves in another stone chamber, one that had four passages leading out of it. Just as they were trying to figure out which passage would lead them to Mr. Joi, they heard the voice of the kind guard echo out from the passage on the far left. 'You know, we shouldn't be made to stand guard at the mouth of that passage with the broken arch. The draft of cold air that flows down that passage from the courtyard outside is not welcoming at all. It's much nicer on this side. I hate that we've been posted there at that very spot every day.'

As they heard the other two guards laugh at the comment, the young friends swiftly made their way down another dark, narrow passage – the one with the broken arch.

The further they walked into the passage, the darker it got. The sound of their breathing and the nervous shuffle of their footsteps echoed in the stone tunnel. The air was damp and still. Kadis hated the darkness, and the feeling of claustrophobia. He stopped and rested his back against the wall. He felt he was choking. The very next instant, he felt a hand hold his. The same hand that had held his a few weeks earlier when he was at the far end of the Kingdom, touring with his father. Sara's hand. He took a deep breath and started moving forward again. Suddenly, they felt a welcome draft of cold air fill their lungs. They must be close to the mouth of the passage. They rushed forward with renewed vigour. A short while later, moonlight filtered into the passageway and they saw the gate beyond. But when Kadis tried to push it open he found to his dismay that it was locked ... and there was no one waiting for them.

⊰ 30 ⊱

Kadis stepped back from the gate. Shijo called out softly, 'Mr. Joi? Hello? You there?'

But there was no answer from the courtyard outside. Just as they were beginning to panic, they heard a grating metallic sound behind them. Startled and afraid, they turned to look inside the passageway but saw nothing. Once again, the grating sound made them jump, but this time they saw the flicker of a flaming torch emerge from the floor, just a few feet away and then a bald, round head.

'Ah, there you are my friends ... and here I am, you see!'

Mr. Joi! They hurried towards him and saw that he had moved aside the manhole cover of some crevice below. He was standing on a ladder with a smile of relief spread over his chubby face. 'Here, follow me down this ladder. Quick!'

His head disappeared below before they could ask any questions. Kadis peered downwards to see Mr. Joi climbing down the ladder. Just before he set his feet on the ground, he looked up and said, 'Come on down, Your Majesty. This will lead us under the courtyard and out the other end, you see. Please make haste!'

And make haste they did. They swiftly climbed down the ladder till they were all at the bottom.

'Follow me,' said Mr. Joi with an enthusiasm that belied the situation they were in.

'Some people are funny, they revel in the adventure of danger,' thought Kadis to himself. 'What a turn my life has taken in these past few weeks. Only time will tell if it has been a turn for the better or for the worse.'

They soon found that this tunnel was even narrower than the ones they had been in.

Mr. Joi stopped after what seemed an eternity. In front of them was a tall steel ladder. He smiled and gestured to the young friends to climb up. 'Up and away!' He himself would go last.

It was quite a distance up. Kadis swallowed nervously at the prospect of climbing the rusty ladder when Sara looked into his eyes and said reassuringly, 'I'm right behind you.'

As he climbed up the precarious ladder, he heard Mr. Joi whisper from below, 'When you reach up, hit the manhole cover three times with your fist. One of my crew will slide it open, you see.'

On reaching the top, Kadis hit the cover as instructed. Shortly after, the cover slid open, and a face popped right over his and said, 'This way, sire!' Kadis heaved himself up. He was swiftly whisked away into the shadows of some trees by another young lad, presumably an additional member of Mr. Joi's spy crew. He was soon followed by his three friends and then a short while later by a huffing Mr. Joi himself.

31

They all stood in silence for a few minutes, breathing in the fresh air. Finally, Mr. Joi broke the silence, 'So now to get you all to the safe house, you see. We have two carriages waiting at the other end of the cluster of trees. You get in the first one and my two helpers will follow in the carriage behind as extra security, you see. On the way there, my helpers will make a quick detour to pick up the sword from Myo's quarters—as explained by you— and hasten to be with you on the way to the safe house.'

'But what about you, Mr. Joi?' asked a concerned Kadis. 'When we're found missing all hell will break loose and if any of it leads back to you then you'll be in trouble.'

'You won't be found missing for a while at least, you see. The duty of checking on you will be undertaken by my contact at the dungeon, the one who left your door unlocked. Every two hours he'll go down to your cell to take a look. And even though none of you will be inside, he'll report back that everything is in order. He'll be able to do this for his entire shift. His shift, however, will be over at sunrise. We only have a few hours left. And don't you worry about me, you see. I have to get back to my station and pretend I know nothing about anything. When my shift is over, I'll make my way over to the safe house once I'm sure that no one is following me. And then I'll prepare to send you all back to the safety of Kofu, the same way you came. All this before you're found to be missing. We only have a limited amount of time, you see, so let's get moving.'

As he turned to leave, he was held back by Kadis. 'Now wait a minute there, Mr. Joi. You just said you are to help us make our way back to Kofu. But that wasn't the plan. We were to find a way to return the sword and stop the war!'

'But you see, I have express instructions from Shonin himself,' protested Mr. Joi.

Kadis protested right back. 'And I've given him our word that we will be successful in our mission, no matter what. Having come so far and gone through so much danger, I'm not about to go back on my word, even if my granduncle himself has instructed you.'

It wasn't just his friends who were surprised by his bold

statement, Kadis was too. Mr. Joi was speechless.

'No more talk of retreating. First, we retrieve the sword, then we head to the safe house to regroup and plan our future course of action,' said Kadis firmly.

Before Mr. Joi or anyone else could refute him, Kadis started walking determinedly towards the carriages. Stunned by the change that had overcome Kadis, the other three stood in silence for a few moments and then rushed to join him.

A few minutes into the journey, the second carriage made the proposed detour to Myo's home. Being part of the castle guard,

Mr. Joi's helpers could enter the castle complex without arousing suspicion. Under cover of darkness, one of the helpers broke into Myo's home through the window while the other stood guard outside. He soon spotted the tattered old sack which held the sword. As he jumped back out of the window into the darkness, the bag glowed radiantly. They peered inside curiously. The bejewelled handle was sparkling brighter than the stars in the night sky. Afraid that the glow from the sword would reveal them, one of the young guards wrapped his overcoat around the sack before jumping onto the waiting carriage.

The two carriages made it back to the safe house without incident. Kadis and his friends entered the house and collapsed from exhaustion. It had been a long day and they were just happy to be alive. On seeing the tattered sack being brought in all aglow, his friends looked at Kadis and smiled proudly. The light of his bravery shone through the sword. Still smiling, the four friends fell into a deep slumber while the two young guards stood outside, keeping watch. They were safe.

For now.

32

An hour later, Mr. Joi rushed into the safe house shouting, 'They've found out! They've found out!'

The four friends woke up with a start, trying to make sense of what was happening in their sleepy, dazed state. Mr. Joi had stormed back to the safe house as soon as he got to know that the young prisoners were discovered missing. It wouldn't be long before groups of soldiers were swarming all over the Kingdom looking for them. The authorities might also get wind of Mr. Joi's involvement in the entire enterprise. He and the young spies were now on borrowed time.

'Please, Your Majesty, I implore you to take my advice and allow me to get you out of the borders of this Kingdom within the next few hours. Security will be tightened around the border areas as soon as news reaches them, you see. We should get going now and beat the news bearers to it.'

Kadis took a deep breath and looked straight into Mr. Joi's eyes. 'I agree with you that we should get going right away ...'

Mr. Joi looked relieved at the young Prince's decision. For that matter, so did the friends. Though they too wanted to go through with the mission, the prospect of the entire army of Molonga being on alert for them seemed too dangerous. It might be wiser to get back to the safety of Kofu and devise another plan of action under Shonin's guidance.

'Where is Mr. Shonin anyway?' asked Sara.

Mr. Joi wiped his brow, 'You see, it will be difficult for him to sneak into Molonga. He sent me word that ... wait, let me read it to you ...'

He took out a small rolled-up piece of paper. 'He sent me word through his falcon.'

He cleared his throat and read it out.

'At this very difficult time, only my young soldiers of peace can appraise the situation you all are in. I, being on the outside and far away from you at this moment, won't be able to judge correctly what it's like in Molonga right now. Therefore, I leave the decision on how to proceed to the capable mind of my grandnephew Kadis. Whether he decides to flee back to Kofu or to plough on and surmount all the mountains of obstacles he might face in Molonga, I'm confident that whichever path he deems fit to follow will be the right one. Either way, I am immensely proud of him and his friends to have bravely gotten so far. Godspeed!'

All eyes were now on Kadis. He took a deep breath and announced to all present, 'Since my very wise granduncle has left the decision to me, then so be it. My decision is as follows. We have not come so far to give up. Our situation might be precarious, but our determination has to be steady as a rock.'

'But you see, when I implied we should swiftly make our way back to Kofu, didn't you just agree with me and say we should get going?' asked a confused Mr. Joi.

'When I said earlier that we should get going, I meant let's get to Tara, and with her help let's take this fight to the lion's den. Let's go with her to King Toki and say what's in our hearts to him with utmost sincerity. Then we humbly hand over the sword as a symbol of peace and love from Kofu. If we can do that, I'm sure that he will see reason. He has to.'

For a moment, Kadis seemed to glow even brighter than the sword itself. Inspired by his determination, they all looked at Mr. Joi and said almost in one voice, 'We are with Kadis!'

Mr. Joi smiled at the young soldiers and said, 'In that case, let's find a way to get to Princess Tara!' There was an unmistakable note of pride in his voice.

Then Myo spoke up. 'I know a way to get to her,' she said. 'Having been her companion for a long time now, I know her routine. At dawn, every day, she takes her favourite horse for a ride in the private forest behind the castle. As the woods are within the castle grounds she only has her guard Binko with her, who follows on horseback. After her ride, she leads her horse to a stream there for a refreshing drink of spring water. Binko never accompanies her to the stream but instead waits a short distance away in the clearing outside. If we can get to that stream in the wooded area before dawn, then we might be able to talk to her while she's all alone.'

Everyone was deep in thought when Kadis voiced a concern. 'The plan itself sounds great once we reach the stream in the woods. The problem is how do we get from *here* to *there* with all the guards looking for us? Any suggestions?'

Kadis turned to Mr. Joi, who had started to pace up and down the length of the room. A few minutes later he stopped and looked back at them. 'There is a way! A few hours before dawn, you see, there's a small caravan of about six horse carriages that enter the castle grounds every day. They carry the produce and dairy from the surrounding farms for everyone within the castle complex, the royal family included. Since this happens every day, they don't inspect each cart but just check the man in charge of the supplies who sits in the lead carriage. If we can smuggle you all into the last cart, maybe you can slip into the grounds unnoticed, you see. And then from there Myo can lead you to the stream.'

'Hmmm ... but how do we get ourselves onto the last carriage?' asked Sara.

Mr. Joi started pacing again and a few moments later said, 'The carriages are loaded in a farming village not far from here. But they will be on their way right now. We won't be able to smuggle you into the carts at the village, you see. If we hurry, we can perhaps intercept them on the way before they reach the castle gates.'

'And how will you intercept the carriages?' Kadis asked.

Mr. Joi shook his head. 'I'm not really sure, you see.'

Everyone looked disappointed. Then suddenly, Kadis picked up the old sack and announced, 'Let's be on our way. We don't have the luxury of time, my dear friends. Mr. Joi will have to plan our next move on the way.'

Kadis walked out of the door, leaving the others no choice but to follow.

'Well, I guess that's decided then. No pressure though ...' said Sara to Mr. Joi with a smile.

'No pressure indeed, you see!' Mr. Joi replied.

33

The four friends were waiting outside when Mr. Joi joined them.

'We'll have to hurry. It won't be too long before the caravan reaches the castle gates. Luckily, we will be under cover of darkness, you see. And we must be vigilant. The castle guards will all be out looking for you. I know a way we can get to a small, wooded area before the road bends towards the castle. It will an arduous trek. I'll lead the way, the four of you follow, but stay close together. We'll leave our guards here as the smaller our party is, the less conspicuous we will be. Please stay close to the trees and bushes and be mindful of any sounds or anything that seems unusual. We don't want to be caught unawares and land up in the dungeon again, you see.'

The motley crew made swift progress and soon found themselves at the foot of some hills. 'Now we'll have to make our way up this rugged hill, you see. Once at the top, we must make a dash for it as there's a large patch of clear ground before we hit the woods. This clear ground also has a pathway that connects the palace grounds to the villages and is used by the guards so we must be very careful. On the other side of the woods is a smaller pathway used by the supply carts to enter the castle grounds. That's where we'll intercept the carriages. I'll lead the way.'

'But Mr. Joi, won't the guards check every carriage now that

there's an alert for us?' asked Sara.

'The guards are on the alert for four fugitives who are trying to escape from Molonga ... not for four fugitives who are trying to get back into the King of Molonga's castle. Follow me!'

Mr. Joi soon began the hike up the hill. Just a few steps in, he turned around and warned, 'Oh, and watch out for the thorny bushes and the steep gradient up ahead.'

A short while later, Myo found her foot caught in the thorny bushes that Mr. Joi had just warned them about. The dark didn't help her cause.

'Oww!' She let out a short scream and fell to the ground. It was a bad scratch. The friends gathered around her and lifted her up.

They still had quite a bit of the climb ahead of them. The friends urged her to try to move on. Shijo rushed to her side. 'Don't you worry, Myo, I'll be by your side and will carry you to safety if I have to.'

Sara found herself smirking and whispered, 'I'm sure he would love that.'

'Come on, please make haste!' cried out Mr. Joi, urgently.

A few strenuous minutes later, the group found themselves almost at the top of the hill. Mr. Joi lifted his head over the edge to get a good view of the clearing. What he saw drained the colour from his face. The place was teeming with troops. He quickly lowered himself. Mr. Joi's expression was a dead giveaway. Kadis hoisted himself to the same vantage point as Mr. Joi and took a good look at the road above. He then came back down and said, 'I noticed the soldiers are moving in small groups. I have a feeling they would all be dispersing from somewhere up the road in groups to look for us. If we see any large group, that would mean those soldiers are heading to the main army base near the border to prepare for battle. We have darkness as our ally – and one more very important factor in our favour ...'

Everyone looked at him expectantly. 'When one group passes above here, it's a while before the next group follows. There is a sharp curve in the trail which probably leads to the main castle grounds from where these troops are marching out. Thanks to that sharp bend in the road, we would have a small window of opportunity to cross before the other group rounds the bend. As soon as one group walks by above, one by one we would have to make a quick dash into the woods beyond, as silently as possible. I do hope there will be enough time for all of us to make it across. Shijo, I think you should be the first to make that dash, followed by Sara, then Mr. Joi and Myo who will go together, and last will be me.'

'Last? Why would you go last?' asked Sara, her voice full of concern.

'Well, someone has to. I'd rather it be me than any one of you,' Kadis replied bravely.

Sara quietly put her hand on his. Kadis looked up and for a brief moment their eyes met. He tightened his grip around her hand and nodded, almost assuring her that he would be alright. Unbeknownst to Sara, Kadis derived most of his strength from her comforting presence.

34

Shijo was the first to make a dash for the woods. He scrambled over as fast as he could and within a few seconds he had made it to the perimeter trees. He paused to catch his breath and then signalled that he was safe. Kadis was keeping watch. Just then another group of soldiers turned the corner and passed by above them. Sara took a deep breath and as silently as she could, sprinted across, making even better time than Shijo. Two down, three to go. Mr. Joi and Myo readied themselves. As soon as it was time, they got up and started running. Myo limped a few paces ahead when Mr. Joi tripped over a pile of rocks and went hurtling across the dusty trail. By then Myo was nearly behind the line of trees. As she turned to help Mr. Joi, the next group of soldiers could be heard as they were about to come into view. Mr. Joi gestured to Myo to hide behind the line of trees. Kadis and the others held their breath while he cleverly lay still and low, close to the very pile of rocks that he had tripped over.

The group of soldiers passed him by, and did not notice the very large rock besides the smaller pile of rocks. As the soldiers went ahead, Kadis got up and dashed towards Mr. Joi, quickly helping him up and pushing him behind the line of trees.

'A close shave indeed, you see!' was the only thing Mr. Joi could say once his breathing had returned to normal.

The group gathered their wits and made their way across the woods as quickly and silently as they could. Mr. Joi assured them that they were still in time to intercept the carriages.

The young friends watched the caravan pass by from behind a clump of trees. As the last carriage came into view, Mr. Joi picked up a pebble and aimed it at the driver of that last carriage where it found its mark smack on the man's head. The friends ducked for cover, convinced that the fall on the army pathway had temporarily affected Mr. Joi's power of rational thought.

But Mr. Joi had his reasons. 'The last carriage driver, you see, is one of my crew!'

He then stepped out of the line of trees and whistled a distinctive sound. The carriage driver turned towards him and on noticing the rotund silhouette of Mr. Joi, smiled and slowed down his carriage. Mr. Joi smirked at his young friends with the look of a man who knew what he was doing.

The friends leapt onto the carriage and hid behind the produce it was carrying. Mr. Joi was the last to board. As he heaved himself onto the carriage, the service gate of the castle creaked open and the first carriage began to make its way in. The carriage driver slowed down to greet the gatekeeper and was waved through without any fuss. A guard was assigned to escort the caravan to the kitchens. He walked at the front by the lead carriage. Within minutes the last carriage had entered the castle grounds.

'After going through all that trouble of getting out of here, we find ourselves back in the lion's den. Oh, the irony of it all!' observed Kadis.

The very next moment, Mr. Joi popped his head above the sacks of potatoes. 'Get ready to jump off at my signal.'

He peeked out through the little opening in the side of the carriage and lifted his hand. As the carriage turned right on the trail towards the castle kitchens, he dropped his hand and whispered urgently, 'Into the woods!'

Without a moment's pause, Kadis hurled himself out of the carriage. He tumbled over and leapt behind the trees. Sara followed soon after, then came Myo, helped down by Shijo. When they looked back, they saw Mr. Joi struggling to get out of the carriage. As he leapt out clumsily, he landed with a sharp thud on the muddy trail. The guard at the front heard the thud and waved at the caravan to halt. He walked briskly towards the source of the sound and spotted Mr. Joi trying to stand up. Mr. Joi noticed the guard approaching and signalled to the young spies to make a run for it and head to the designated spot. At first the group of friends stood their ground but another more forceful gesture by Mr. Joi made them realize the seriousness of the situation. Reluctantly, they turned and started to run. They could hear the faint sound of the stream in the distance.

The guard stopped near the fallen heap of a man and firmly helped him up. He was surprised to see Mr. Joi there and whistled to the guards at the gate, who promptly ran to the spot. The carriage men too peeped out to see what was going on. The head guard at the service gate recognized Mr. Joi.

'Sir, I'm sorry but you will have to accompany us. There's a search order out for you.'

With these words, the head guard firmly held his arm and led him away.

35

The young runaways soon reached the designated spot. The capture of Mr. Joi had left them with a feeling of despair. Sensing the general mood, Kadis addressed the gathering with a resolute tone in his voice, 'I understand what you all are going through because I too am feeling the same. Mr. Joi's capture was most unfortunate. But now is the crucial moment that will decide victory or defeat. Very soon the Princess will arrive here and if we're to succeed in our lofty mission, we must stick to our plan and speak to her. If she's on our side, then I'm sure she'll try and do what she can to free Mr. Joi once we're able to put a stop to the hostilities and end the possibility of war.'

A short while later, they heard the neighing of a horse. The Princess had arrived. They peeped through the bushes to see her lead her horse to the stream. As she sat on a nearby tree stump, she heard some footsteps behind her. Startled, she jumped up and was about to call out to her guard Binko when she saw Kadis and the others. Her first reaction was one of relief as she ran towards them and gave them a collective hug.

'I'm so glad you all are safe,' Tara said. 'How did you get here?'

Kadis replied, 'We have a lot to tell you but that can wait. Right now, there are more pressing matters. We know that your father King Toki and your uncle General Seiya are gathering the troops

at the army camp. The navy too is readying their ships. Not long from now, both will be ready for battle and will be given the order to proceed towards Kofu. The armies there are already preparing for the attack and will be ready and waiting. Whoever wins, the real fallout will be the loss of many precious lives on both sides and misery for all. Tara, we have to stop that, now! We need to get to your father and I have to give him this sword as a gesture of peace from Kofu.'

Kadis lifted the old sack and showed Tara the mystical sword. It was glowing even brighter than when Kadis had first shown it to her. Tara held the sword that had been the bone of contention between the two Kingdoms for so long. Then Kadis said, 'I'm sure with you by our side we will be able to convince them to stop the advance of the troops and to initiate a meaningful, peaceful dialogue with Kofu. In their hearts, I am sure the two Kings, our fathers, would rather have peace than war. And one more thing, our friend Mr. Joi has been arrested for helping us. We implore you to do everything in your power to free him.'

Tara was silent for a few moments and then enveloped her cousin Kadis in a tight embrace. 'What you all have done here is so brave! I'm with you on this noble mission. We don't have much time left but we must do all within our means to succeed. Wait right here while I get Binko.'

Tara ran out towards the clearing and soon returned with her guard in tow. 'I've explained the situation to Binko as best and as quickly as I could. He'll help us today.'

Binko smiled and said, 'What I know is that since the Royal Guard have made the arrest, they would have to bring him to the King's court right away. But since His Highness King Toki himself is at the army camp, they will take the arrested person to the King wherever he might be.'

'Hmm ... so that means everyone will be at one place. We'll have the opportunity to convince King Toki to stop the war and release Mr. Joi too,' said Kadis.

'Sadly, it won't be simple to convince my father and uncle, I can tell you that. And if any one of them or the senior officers lose their cool on seeing you all, as you all are branded as spies and the enemy, we'll be in trouble!' added Tara.

'That's alright. It only means we need to get our point across to the King before anyone else can,' Sara said, trying to keep their hopes up.

'Easier said than done,' sighed Myo knowingly.

'Easier dead than …' started Shijo before a stern look from Kadis shut him up.

And so they were on their way again. Binko knew a short cut through the dense forest on the other side of the stream. With Binko in the lead, the group slowly made their way downhill.

The now steady iridescence of the sword helped quash any feelings of fear that might have wanted to surface.

After a long walk, the group reached the edge of the forest. Up ahead was a steep descent. They could see the Molongan forces below– lines of soldiers, horses, weapons and tents.

'We must make our way closer to the army camp below. And then with Tara's help we need to locate her father and General Seiya. She's the Princess after all, so no one will stop her from meeting her own father and uncle – if she can only bring the two of them to meet us at a designated spot. The rest is up to fate,' Kadis said with authority.

'I know a narrow track that leads down towards the camp. We'll wait for darkness to fall and then make our way down. The descent will take about two hours,' said Binko.

'The moment we have been waiting for is here,' Kadis declared.

❧ 36 ❧

A few hours later, the sun slowly started to dip beneath the distant horizon. Darkness soon took over the sky, save for a few errant rays of moonlight that managed to seep through the heavy cloud cover.

In the next hour, they cautiously made their way to the halfway mark. From here on it was going to be a steep descent with large rocks for cover. With Binko leading the way, they slowly made their way downhill in the dark, on a narrow, winding and precipitous path. Kadis held on tightly to the sack which housed the precious sword. They were moving very slowly for if they slipped it would be a rough tumble all the way down into the enemy camp. Suddenly, Shijo uttered a sharp cry. He had tripped over a small rock and was struggling to keep his balance. Kadis leapt to his rescue and held on to him as did Sara and Myo who were behind him. But, in that one moment of trying to rescue his friend the young Prince had inadvertently let go of the sack. Shijo had been rescued in the nick of time, but the sack tumbled down the rocky hillside.

No sooner had Shijo been rescued, than Kadis realized what had happened. They stood dumbfounded as they saw the sack with the sword roll and bounce down the hillside. It gathered speed as it neared the bottom of the hill. And then just a few feet above the ground, it crashed into a rock and came to a stop. A lone soldier looked up towards the source of the sound but seeing nothing, resumed his duties. Retrieving the sword seemed almost impossible.

Sara finally spoke, after a few moments of stunned silence, 'On the bright side, that rock just saved our lives. I suggest we all continue down as planned. Once we get to the spot that Binko wants to take us, Princess Tara can stealthily make her way to the camp and find her father. While we wait for her to return, we will find a way to retrieve the sword.'

'How can we proceed as planned?! We must first get the sword and only then should we go ahead,' said a harried Shijo.

Kadis put his hand up authoritatively to stop any further discussion on the matter.

'Sara is right. We don't have much time. It won't remain dark for much longer. If we don't retrieve the sword all will be lost anyway, as once we are revealed to General Seiya he might not give us a chance to get to the sword. We must proceed as planned.'

They soon continued down the precarious pathway. Then, as the track turned, they found themselves on a landing. As they sat down to rest, Binko ushered Kadis around a corner of the hillside. He then climbed nearly fifteen feet up the steep hill face and asked Kadis to follow. From that vantage point Binko pointed to the path Kadis could take to get to the sword. 'Sire, as soon as I leave with the Princess, you should carefully make your way to the sword on this path and retrieve it before our return.'

After Tara and Binko left for the camp, Kadis took charge, determined to overcome the obstacles that lay ahead. Trying not to show his fear and anxiety, he said, 'Myo, I think you should stay here at the landing to keep watch in case we are spotted – and for when Tara returns. Sara and Shijo, I'll need you to climb up with me to the spot from where we can see the rock by which lies the sword. Shijo can stay at the top to keep a lookout for both Myo and me. Sara, you can guide me from a vantage point that I will show you.'

Without any further ado and with full faith in the words of their friend and leader, they all did as instructed. Myo stayed back by herself to keep watch. Shijo was the first to climb up the fifteen-foot-high rock face and put out his hand for Sara. Kadis brought up the rear. It wasn't an easy climb, but they all made it to the top. Step one was successfully taken.

Once the three had made it to the top of the rock face, Shijo crouched down to keep watch. When Sara and Kadis got to the next vantage point, Shijo pointed to the rock where the sword lay. It was a steep and rough climb down. Kadis would have to crawl on all-fours to avoid being seen. Sara could never have imagined that someday Kadis would undertake such a perilous task.

Down at the army camp below, Tara tried to walk nonchalantly through the army camp towards her father. Word had reached him just a short while ago that the Princess and her loyal guard Binko were nowhere to be seen after their morning horse ride. He was starting to get concerned about her whereabouts even though his trusted guard was with her. As Tara and Binko walked through the ranks of soldiers they could see General Seiya's tent at a distance. But they needed to go directly to King Toki. She trusted her father to understand what she had to say more than she trusted her uncle, who was always ready to go into battle at a moment's notice.

******

Up on the craggy hill, Kadis set out towards the sword. He would have to crawl on the rough surface all the way there and back without being seen. As he inched forward slowly—his knees and hands getting bruised by the rough surface—the voices from the camp below became louder. He cast a worried look towards Sara. After several tense moments, Kadis was finally close to the rock. Sara signalled to Shijo that Kadis had reached the sword. Kadis stretched out his arm towards the sword. It was just out of reach. He crawled forward a little bit more. But, just as he grabbed the sack, he inadvertently pushed the rock against which it had been resting. The rock went bouncing down the hillside and fell with a thud near the foot of the lone soldier stationed at the bottom of the hill. Kadis and Sara felt their hearts stop for a moment. Kadis flattened himself against the hillside, and covered his head with the scruffy brown sack, and lay very still.

******

Tara and Binko walked through the camp silently. Getting through unnoticed was proving to be quite an impossible task for the young Princess. The soldiers knew who she was and immediately bowed in respect when they saw her. Suddenly, they spotted General Seiya's imposing figure outside his tent.

'Binko ... do you see what I'm seeing?'

'Yes, Your Highness, I can see General Seiya. What do you suggest?' asked the loyal Binko.

'I suggest that we make a dash for it! Lead the way please, will you, Binko?'

And they were off like two horses at a race. It was a strange sight indeed to see a young royal and her old loyal running through the army ranks. One of General Seiya's officers did, however, catch a fleeting glimpse.

'General, if I am not mistaken, I did notice the Princess running that way,' he said, pointing towards that side.

'The Princess? Here? HMMPHH! She must have been found, I suppose. Highly irregular behaviour, I must add. I need to speak with the young girl's father about disciplining her. Come on!'

'But, sir, if I may, now is hardly the time ...' the officer tried to interject.

'HMMPHH! It's always the time to drill some discipline into young people!'

General Seiya immediately started to make his way towards his brother-in-law's tent.

******

Back on the hill, Kadis remained perfectly still. The rock had fallen next to a soldier who looked upwards at once. But, when he couldn't see anything in the dark, he began to climb the hill. Sara held her breath. She could see the soldier getting closer to Kadis. When he was just a couple of feet away, he stopped and looked around. All he could see was grey rocks and brown mud. The moon was under cloud cover, so it was difficult to see clearly. Not noticing anything amiss, the soldier took one last look and started to go back down. Sara let out a long sigh of relief. Kadis turned towards Sara, who gestured that the coast was clear. Kadis started to make his way back with the brown canvas sack firmly in his hand.

❦ 38 ❧

Tara and Binko spotted the decorated tent of King Toki a short distance away and rushed towards it. The guards bowed respectfully and parted the curtain of the tent to let in the running Princess. King Toki stood in battle gear inside the tent, deep in discussion with a senior army officer. A tall and slim man, he sported a thin moustache that made him look stern and grim. When he saw Tara enter, he rushed towards her and enveloped her in a warm embrace.

'Where in god's name were you? Why did you not go back home after your morning ride?' he demanded.

Before she could answer, he turned to Binko, 'Binko, I expected you to be more responsible. You know we're on the brink of war and at a time like this you're supposed to make sure the Princess doesn't deviate from her routine. This mustn't ...' Before he could finish, Tara spoke up, 'Father, I'm safe and sound so please don't worry! I need to speak to you right away in private about where I was and why I didn't come home after my ride.'

'Tara, whatever it is, it will have to wait. This is not the time ...'

But, Tara insisted, 'It can't wait, father. It's a matter of the utmost urgency!'

Sensing the serious tone in her voice, King Toki signalled to the army officer to step outside. He then sat down to listen to what

Tara had to say.

In the meantime, General Seiya had been swiftly making his way to the King's tent when he was stopped by some officers wanting to discuss the upcoming battle.

*****

On the hill, clinging tightly to the sack, Kadis slowly crawled back to the rock where Sara was waiting, watching his every move and the surroundings with an eagle eye.

They had done it.

Now for the main task at hand.

*****

'So you're trying to tell me that the son of my enemy—whom we are going to attack—is right here by the army camp? My soldiers have orders to arrest the escaped prisoners and they've come right here under our very noses? And they want a word with the very King from whose dungeon they have escaped and who has ordered their arrest?'

King Toki couldn't believe the incredulous story he had just heard from his daughter.

'Please father, I implore you to give them a chance. I'll take you to them but only if you're alone. If you're not convinced or for any reason don't see their point of view, you can have them arrested again. Your army is right here at your command. They won't be able to escape.'

King Toki was deep in thought. He had never refused any

request made by his daughter, but this was something that he couldn't bring himself to do. 'Why would I want to listen to what they have to say? They're the enemy and have escaped from my dungeon. I should have them thrown right back in there!'

'Please trust me, father. I'll never ask you for anything ever again, as long as I live ...' Tara said, beginning to cry.

'Fine. Let's go right now. I'll go with you alone. But if I find anything amiss or suspicious, I'll arrest them myself!'

Tara wrapped her arms around her father.

'Father, you're the best! Please let's leave from the back entrance of your tent.'

A few moments later the General entered the King's tent to find no one there.

'Now where on earth could His Highness have disappeared to? And at a time like this! HMMPH!'

❦ 39 ❧

Myo was keeping watch and jumped up excitedly when she saw King Toki and Tara in the distance. She turned to Shijo and whistled, pointing in the direction of the King. Shijo passed on the message to Sara and Kadis, 'They're approaching!'

A short uphill trek later, King Toki and Tara found themselves on the landing where Myo sat waiting. 'That's it? You've dragged me away from my army to meet just this insolent little girl?'

Then hearing some sounds from above, King Toki looked up to see young Kadis, Shijo and Sara making their way down to him.

King Toki sat himself down on a small boulder. Tara stood by his side. 'You don't have a lot of time, and remember, I can have you thrown back in the dungeon whenever I want and get your father to do my bidding. So, whatever it is you have to say, say it now!' said King Toki sternly.

Kadis cleared his throat nervously and bowed. 'Your Highness, we are very grateful to you for meeting with us. I assure you we aren't spies of any sort. We are not here to report back on whatever it is you are planning. We have come here humbly to put an end to this war ...'

'Let me stop you right here,' King Toki said, 'you will have me believe that the King of Kofu has sent his Prince and some other children to beg me to stop this war? That's not very brave of him, is it now?'

'With all due respect, Your Highness, my father is a very brave man,' Kadis responded to the jibe.

'Well, he's either very brave, or very stupid. I can't say which right now. Time will tell.'

'Your Highness, I recently got to know the story of how the once happy Kingdom of Kofu separated into two Kingdoms. My granduncle told me.'

'Old Shonin is still alive? I didn't know that. I didn't mind him really ... though he wasn't brave enough to take sides in our quarrel.'

'He didn't want to take sides because both were his family. How could he choose one over the other?'

'Well, in a way he did choose, didn't he? He stayed back in Kofu.'

'That was his home. And so was the state of Molonga. But he didn't stay in Kofu, he lived by himself outside the limits of the Kingdom. He has sent us here to make things right. We have come as soldiers of peace.'

King Toki had a look of amazement on his face as he listened keenly to what Kadis was saying.

Kadis continued, 'You see, Your Highness, one quarrel between family members, whatever the reason might be, has divided our families many years since and made strangers, even enemies of us. We are still fighting to justify what our elders were fighting about. It isn't even your argument, nor my father's and neither mine nor my cousin Tara's. But we're paying the price by being on the brink of a blood-soaked war where whoever wins, there will be losses on both sides. Losses of the lives of people who in their heart want nothing more than a time of peace where they can be with their families and work for their happiness. All that will be taken away for the sake of justifying a quarrel from many years ago. You will attack Kofu, my father will defend it and there will be hundreds—no, thousands—of lives lost before the outcome is decided. Now tell me what sort of victory would that be?'

'You won't understand, boy. What do you know of family honour? You're from Kofu after all! Enough of this talk!' King Toki said dismissively.

He then stood up, for he was done listening to a discourse on peace from a young boy.

But, Kadis still had to make his most important move. 'I have something for you, Your Highness. An offering of peace ...' He gently picked up the old sack and presented it to King Toki.

'How insolent can you be, boy? I am a King, and you gift me a tattered old canvas bag? It's time to have you thrown back in the dungeon.'

He turned to walk away when Kadis said, 'Your Highness, you shouldn't deride a treasure just because the sack is dirty, just as you shouldn't dismiss what we have to say because we are young.'

King Toki noticed a glow emanating from the sack. He paused for a moment.

'Could it be ...?' he thought to himself.

Kadis gently pulled out the sword. It shone like a jewel, just like it would have in its days of glory.

'Here is the sword that was the pride of the family. It had been preserved by granduncle Shonin and today it's back where it rightfully belongs ... in your hands.'

King Toki took the magnificent sword, inspecting it closely as he held it, feeling its power.

'How did you get possession of the sword? Does your father know about this? Because if he doesn't, then that would only mean he's still hostile towards Molonga!'

There was silence amongst the young solders. They were stumped as they weren't official emissaries of the King of Kofu. In fact, he had no idea they were even here! After a few moments Kadis cleared his throat, 'Um, Your Highness ... my father, His Majesty King Rissho actually sent us here as soldiers of peace. He knew he wouldn't be welcome here but if we made it, he trusted the goodness of the people of Molonga to not harm young souls, even if they might come from an enemy Kingdom ...'

Kadis had lied and his friends knew it, but they also understood that a lie that can save thousands of lives is sometimes worthier than the truth.

The King of Molonga, visibly moved, sat down. 'B-but I always thought of him as hostile towards us and here he sent young innocent children to my country believing in our goodness. The sword, it ... it was glowing when you held it! I had heard of the legend that if the sword was used against loved ones it would lose its sheen and would only ever glow again in the hands of ... of a true soldier of peace, and the future true King of a united kingdom. When I heard that legend, I thought it was as impossible to meet someone who could make this sword glow as seeing a ship fly! And now ... right here in front of my eyes I see the very sword of my ancestors ... glowing in your hands ...'

Completely overwhelmed, the King sat still for a few moments, just gazing at the sword. Then, composing himself, he stood up. 'So the legend is true then ...'

He turned to Kadis. 'You are the soldier of peace and the true future King!'

Kadis bowed respectfully to King Toki.

'Your Highness, we must stop the war. I know that General Seiya will be tough to convince but we must.'

King Toki smiled warmly at Kadis. He then turned to the rest and bowed humbly.

'I salute your bravery. I believe we have a war to stop!'

The young soldiers let out a cheer of joy and relief. Princess Tara ran to her father and gave him a tight hug.

'I love you, father!'

He hugged her back and smiled.

'Let's go!'

❦ 40 ❧

'Where is that brother-in-law of mine? Where is the King? HMMPH!' General Seiya ranted as he paced about restlessly.

Then he mounted his horse and rode to the front lines of the army. On the far right stood the cage in which Mr. Joi had been imprisoned.

General Seiya addressed the ranks. 'Before we set out to quash the so-called Kingdom of Kofu we must punish this man on the right. Joi was my officer who was assigned the task of training young cadets to become capable soldiers. Instead, he raised an army of young spies. Death will be his only reward. I hereby sentence him to be hanged!'

On hearing his sentence, poor Mr. Joi fell to the floor and started to pray.

The General's next in command said in his ear, 'General, I think only His Highness the King has the right to sentence any prisoner to death.'

'HMMPH! I'm aware of that! Only the King has the right to sentence the spy and only the King has the right to command the troops to proceed for war. BUT WHERE IS THE KING?!' he screamed out.

'Can no one find him? Has he run away? The law says that since

I am the King's kin and the General of his armies, I have the power to take over command should the King be absent in his duties!'

He haughtily rode his horse parallel to the front lines of the army, 'I hereby declare war on Kofu! I order our brave soldiers to resolutely defeat the enemy and come back victorious! Let us begin with the hanging of the spy. And once his band of young spies is found by our elite squad, they too will meet the same fate!' roared the General.

The lines of army officers roared back.

Just as he was about to signal for Mr. Joi to be taken out of his cage, a loud voice was heard, 'STOP! I COMMAND IT!!'

General Seiya looked around.

'Who dare command the General?'

'It is I, your KING!' roared back King Toki.

General Seiya couldn't believe his eyes. King Toki was walking towards him accompanied by the young spies.

'There are the spies. OFFICERS! ARREST THEM!' General Seiya commanded.

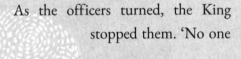

As the officers turned, the King stopped them. 'No one

will touch them. They're not spies but soldiers of peace.'

Enraged, the General dismounted from his horse and walked up to the King in a huff.

'My dear brother-in-law! What is the meaning of this? What is wrong with you? Have these spies brainwashed you? Have they forced you to eat or drink something that has affected your thinking?'

'They haven't brainwashed me but rather made me see sense. I order you to stop this war, General!' King Toki commanded.

General Seiya could not believe what he was hearing. 'I declare the King is not in his senses and that the command be taken over by me! I order my officers to take the King back to his palace and keep him there under house arrest and the spies put in the cage with Joi, to be hanged with him at my command!'

The confused officers didn't know what to do.

Before the General could say anything more, an enraged King Toki gave him a resounding slap! 'You may be General ... but it is MY army that I *let* you command! I'm completely in my senses and COMMAND this war be stopped, with immediate effect. And I want the prisoner Mr. Joi released right now!'

General Seiya stood there with his hand on his cheek, smarting from the slap. King Toki then turned to his officers, 'As your King, I order you to put the General under house arrest until he has been apprised of the situation and comes to his senses.'

He then mounted his horse and like the true King he was, rode majestically down the line of the army ranks.

'AT EASE, SOLDIERS! THE WAR IS OFF! GET BACK TO YOUR TENTS AND AWAIT FURTHER ORDERS!'

41

Later that day, General Seiya was summoned to the King's court. The General sat in his regular position at the court but with two of the King's guard by his side. He noticed the group of young soldiers of peace whom he still thought of as spies, sitting beside the King. Soon after, Mr. Joi was also summoned. As he walked in the young friends ran up and hugged him affectionately.

King Toki stood up to address the gathering. 'Today I have summoned the court for a very special reason. You all must be wondering why I called off the war yesterday. Well, I had reason to and unlike what some people in the room might think,' he said, glancing at his brother-in-law General Seiya, 'I'm completely in my senses.'

General Seiya sheepishly looked at the floor as all eyes turned to him. The King continued, 'Let me introduce you to these brave young people sitting by me. This here is Kadis, the Prince of Kofu and his friends Shijo and Sara, besides of course my daughter Princess Tara and her companion by royal decree, Myo.'

There was a distinct murmur of voices in the court as those gathered there wondered why the King would give the enemy a place of honour. Then King Toki raised his hand. 'Allow me to explain why I am honouring these young people.'

Stepping down from the throne, he walked among the

courtiers as he spoke, 'Many years ago, our families were united but due to some misunderstandings and mistrust the family elders had a terrible quarrel that led to violence. The sword of the state of Molonga, which was a part of Kofu then, was taken away and the families became bitter enemies. Our uncle Shonin did try several times to broker peace but we would have none of it. The state of Molonga separated from Kofu and was then declared an independent Kingdom. That didn't go down well with Kofu and several skirmishes and smaller battles took place. As the years passed by, the enmity between the two grew stronger even though King Rissho and I have never quarrelled amongst ourselves. We were merely carrying on the quarrel of our elders from many years ago. I don't think many of the citizens of Molonga or even Kofu for that matter know what that quarrel was about. Well, it doesn't really matter, does it? What matters is the present moment.'

The people gathered at the court were listening intently to the King. 'Just like we have our informants planted in Kofu, they too had their people assimilated into our society to pass on vital information to them, Mr. Joi being one of the few.'

Everyone turned to look at Mr. Joi who shifted uncomfortably in his seat.

'Well, he is nothing but a patriot to his cause and if he was from Molonga these very qualities would be honoured here at this court.'

King Toki walked back to his royal seat and sat down before adding, 'It was these young boys and girls here who took up the mantle of ending the hostilities between the two countries. From what I've been told, King Rissho trusted our better nature to not put them to serious harm if we discovered their true intent.'

Kadis squirmed in his seat on hearing this, then thought to himself, 'If the white lie is going to be instrumental in bringing about peace, then it was worth it.'

'HMMPH!' the General said loudly. 'It's cowardice, that's what this is! Kofu trying to run scared from facing us!'

King Toki disdainfully looked at General Seiya for a while before addressing the court again. 'These young soldiers of peace have told me that this is what the King of Kofu dreamed of. Even as he prepares for battle with us, he aspires for peace. Some of you may construe that as being weak or being scared. The fact that he has bravely sent his own son, the young Prince here to return the sword shows his bravery and his trust that we will respond to his gesture by agreeing to peace.'

'What? He has come to return the sword? The Sword of Molonga?'

General Seiya couldn't believe what he had just heard. King Toki smiled and gestured to his aide, who came hurriedly to his side with the tattered brown sack. He slowly pulled out the glowing, magnificent sword.

There was a gasp amongst all those present. When the sword was taken away it had lost its sheen and turned dull and unrecognizable. Everyone knew of the legend and couldn't believe that it would come true in their lifetime. Kadis and his friends looked at each other and smiled. The General sprang from his seat and ran to the King's side.

'Please, may I?'

The King nodded. General Seiya took the sword in his own

hands and looked at it with a keen eye, inspecting it from every angle.

'Still suspicious, eh, brother-in-law?' King Toki said with a wicked glint in his eye.

General Seiya looked up at the King. 'It is indeed the sword of our ancestors ... and it has been restored to its former glory! A feat that could only happen when someone very brave with only peace in his heart would bring it back.'

General Seiya then turned to young Prince Kadis. 'I just never thought it would be this scrawny, young Prince from the enemy Kingdom ...'

There was light laughter all around. Kadis too enjoyed the General's feeling of astonishment. General Seiya then walked up to the young Prince and stood imposingly in front of him. He smiled awkwardly. 'Well then, give us a hug, young lad!'

He lifted Kadis up and gave him a very clumsy hug.

One of the ministers stood up and shouted out loud, 'HIP-HIP!'

And the rest joined in, 'HURRAY!'

42

'We did it!' Sara screamed in joy when they were back in their rooms at the Molongan castle.

'Thank you for giving me the courage,' said Kadis to Sara. 'If this plan hadn't worked and if anything had gone wrong, we would all have been languishing in the dungeons as prisoners of war awaiting the gallows. But instead, here we were celebrating the sweet song of victory,' he added happily.

He held her hands and declared, 'You are my strength!'

They stood in silence for a few moments, looking into each other's eyes and then Sara gave him a kiss on his cheek and hugged him tight. 'Thank you for being the way you are ...' she said with a warm smile on her face.

The shy Prince blushed. Emboldened by this display of affection, Shijo too held Myo's hand. Myo smiled back, tightening her grip on his hand. It was now Shijo's turn to blush! Seeing all the love in the air, Mr. Joi smiled affectionately at the young friends.

As they sat eating some refreshments, Kadis suddenly had a look of concern on his face.

'What's the matter?' asked Sara.

Kadis replied, 'We've completed our mission successfully but what of my father? He doesn't know any of this. He's out there at the front lines of Kofu preparing for the biggest battle of his life.

How do we get him to step down? How do we explain and justify this dangerous undertaking of ours? He might even get impatient very soon and launch the attack on Molonga. And if he does, then all this talk of peace will come to naught. He must be apprised of the situation right away! How are we going to tell him about all of this?'

There was silence as everyone pondered the new problem at hand. It was Sara who spoke up first, 'Shonin, of course! We must send word to him right away about our mission's success and about this problem.'

'If you all just wait for ... maybe a few minutes, you see, you could ask him yourself!' said Mr. Joi with a mischievous twinkle in his eye.

'Granduncle Shonin? Here? How? When?' asked Kadis excitedly.

'How about right now?' They heard the familiar baritone from the doorway. Standing there under the arch was Shonin himself. He rushed forward to give his young wards a bear hug. Kadis, Sara and Shijo pounced affectionately on him.

'I'm so proud of my young soldiers. Mission accomplished in a way that even I couldn't have imagined,' said Shonin with a wide smile on his weather-beaten face, adding, 'History will remember you all very fondly.'

He then turned to Tara. 'And I am your granduncle too, you know.'

Tara went up to him shyly and bowed.

'Bless you, my child!' said Shonin affectionately.

'But granduncle, how did you arrive ...' asked Kadis.

'Well, Molonga doesn't consider Kofu the enemy anymore, do they?'

Kadis slapped his forehead, 'Oh yes, of course! That will take some getting used to.'

'On the other hand, I wish I could say the same about Kofu ...'

Kadis grimaced. 'Granduncle ... the thing is ...'

'Look, I know the reason for your white lie. Though not a ruse I would use, it did the trick. Now we have to rectify it because a white lie is only ever a short-term solution.'

'But how can we do that? Could we send word with your falcon?'

'No, that won't do. Your father won't believe such news unless it came from you. And besides, if word reached him that you were in Molonga, whatever the situation might be, he wouldn't believe a scroll carried by a bird. On not finding you in my cottage, he might suspect foul play and march with his forces to initiate an attack on Molonga. We will have to take permission to leave, head to Kofu and tell your father everything.'

'But what if he refuses the idea of peace and gets angry with us for coming here with the sword, without his knowledge and permission?'

'Well, since you were brave enough to fulfil this mission in what was once enemy territory, I'm sure you'll be able to fulfil your new mission in your home territory.'

'B-but ...'

Shonin just smiled at Kadis and the others.

'But it *is* as easy as it sounds!'

Taking leave from King Toki, they prepared to head back. The problem for the young soldiers of peace was that King Toki wanted to follow them with his royal party to meet his long-lost cousin, King Rissho. He had given them just an hour to complete their task: to explain the situation and to convince King Rissho that King Toki was on his way there with peace on his mind.

Kadis sighed as he got ready, 'Easier said than done ...'

Shijo muttered under his breath, 'Easier dead than done!'

❦ 43 ❧

The entourage left Molonga before the break of dawn. They entered Kofu through the secret passage. It was early evening by the time they reached Shonin's cottage. They left their belongings under the care of the wise Shonin, before making their way towards the army camp.

The sight before them confirmed their worst fears. The completed wall looked more imposing with archers in position on top of it. The army was in position to defend the attack from the enemy forces of Molonga. As they approached the King's tents, they saw King Rissho deep in conversation with the General of the Kofu army. Surprised at seeing Kadis and the others there, King Rissho gestured for them to wait while he finished his conversation.

'Your Majesty, all the forces are ready to defend our great Kingdom on both the fronts. And as instructed by you, the Elite soldiers are ready to ambush the lead party from Molonga that will precede their army.'

'Very good, General. Let's teach those Molongans a lesson they will never forget! Keep a lookout for their lead party,' King Rissho commanded, very pleased with the army's preparations.

Kadis' breath quickened. It was not a lead party for the army that would be arriving soon, but rather the peace party of the King of Molonga to celebrate the closure of hostilities. He could not let King Toki get ambushed by the Kofu soldiers. That would be disastrous for peace.

'Father ...' Kadis called out anxiously as he walked towards King Rissho.

'What are you doing here? Why aren't you at your granduncle's cottage? And ...'

'Father, I must interrupt you. It's very urgent!'

'Not now, son, I have very pressing matters to attend to. Later perhaps ...'

'No! I need to talk to you now.'

King Rissho was taken aback by his son's forceful tone of voice.

'What is it that can't wait? Can't you see that we are on the brink of war? What can be more urgent than that?' King Rissho said, sounding annoyed.

'Father, I'll tell you what's more urgent than being on the brink of war.'

'What on earth could that be?'

'Being on the brink of peace.'

King Rissho was speechless on hearing his son speak to him that way.

'Not here, father. I need to talk to you alone, and right now.'

King Rissho nodded and walked towards his tent.

'Father, I beg you, please don't send your soldiers to ambush the lead party. Call it off right now and I'll explain later,' pleaded Kadis.

'What? Have you lost your mind, son? Have you any idea what's going on here?'

'I do, father! Please trust me just this once. Once you've called it off, I promise I'll explain, and it will all be clear to you.'

King Rissho hesitated for a moment. He had never seen his son talk to him like this. Something must definitely be going on and he intended to find out. He called out to his commander-in-chief.

'General!'

'General, I need you to stop the soldiers from leaving ...' King Rissho said as soon as the General entered the tent.

The General looked confused.

'... for now!' the King completed his sentence.

'Yes, Your Majesty.' The General bowed and left the tent, not sure what his King was up to.

✺ 44 ✺

Ving Rissho looked askance at his young son. Kadis took a
deep breath.

'Father, please sit down. I'll be as brief as possible. Granduncle
Shonin, whom you sent us to study and train with ... well, he told us
about the history of the two Kingdoms and how they separated. He
also told us about ... the sword ...'

'What? *The* sword? Why would he tell you children all of this?'

King Rissho already seemed quite upset and Kadis hadn't even
mentioned the mission.

'Father, after we heard the story of how the two families turned
enemies, we were all very saddened. Granduncle Shonin sent us on
a mission ...'

'Mission? What sort of mission? What on earth are you
blabbering about, son?'

He stood up agitatedly. Kadis gestured very humbly for him to
take his seat.

'A mission of peace ...'

'What? Where did he send you on this er ... mission of peace?'

Kadis hesitated for a moment but he knew he had to
continue bravely.

'To ... er ... well ... Molonga!'

'MOLONGA? You went to Molonga? ALONE? Without my

knowledge? That uncle Shonin ... I will ...'

King Rissho had sprung up from his seat again.

'Father! This enmity with Molonga was neither your doing nor King Toki's. It was a family feud started by our ancestors that got out of hand and only escalated with the passage of time. You both had nothing to do with it. You were fighting someone else's battle. So, granduncle explained the matter to us and just like there are soldiers of war, he sent us there as soldiers of peace.'

'That uncle Shonin! He was always an oddball but I never expected him to endanger your lives!'

'But we didn't die, father! I'm here safe and sound, aren't I?'

Kadis had a point. King Rissho took a deep breath to calm himself down. 'Go on then.'

'He has a network of spies there – in important places. We entered Molonga with their help.'

By this point, King Rissho was shaking with rage. Kadis quickly continued his story lest the King interrupt him and harm Shonin or their cause for peace. 'We got in touch with Princess Tara and she understood our point of view and came on our side.'

'So you expect me to believe that the enemy Princess sided with you instead of her own father?'

'Well, she sided with peace. And with her help we met King Toki and reasoned with him. We had carried the sword with us ... and we gave him back the sword, which was the symbol of their side of the family and a bone of contention ever since it was taken away from them.'

'WHAT?! You took the sword with you? How did you get hold

of it? I need to know! Do you even know of the legend of that sword?' asked King Rissho, his voice getting louder every second.

'We were given the sword by granduncle Shonin. And I do know the legend, father ... and by the time it passed from my hands to the King of Molonga, it was all aglow ... just as the legend goes!'

The King was dumbfounded. No one spoke for a few moments. Then Kadis continued.

'After we reasoned with him, King Toki understood what our intentions were and agreed to stop the attack and come and meet you as a gesture of goodwill.'

'The King of Molonga is coming here? Now?'

'Yes, father ... not as an advance party for his army but as a small peace party – he and his daughter Princess Tara are coming here with peace in their hearts.'

King Rissho slowly walked to the corner. He was deep in thought.

'And ... one more thing, father ... well ... I told King Toki that I was there with your blessing and that returning the sword was your idea. I also said that you trusted their better nature so much that you sent your son there unarmed to talk of peace.'

King Rissho listened silently.

'This won him over and he regretted all the

years wasted on war between the two families. He desires only peace from now on. Please, father, welcome peace and let's all live happily again ...' Kadis added.

Pacing up and down the room, King

Rissho tried to process all that he had heard. He looked at Kadis every few moments and couldn't believe how far the once timid boy had come in such a short span of time. He continued pacing and then suddenly, without a word to Kadis, he stepped out of the tent and called out, 'General! I need you to accompany me. We are going forth to meet the advance party from Molonga. And I need the Elite squad with us!'

Kadis came running out. The General was confused.

'But Your Highness, I thought we had decided on sending just the Elite stealthily. Why would we meet them openly and expose ourselves?'

'Because, my dear General, we are not afraid of any King of Molonga or his army!'

In a matter of moments, the Elite squad had assembled. King Rissho and his army General mounted their steeds. The officers gathered around, wondering if this was a wise move. But the King wore a serious expression. He then turned to Kadis. 'What are you looking at, son? Gather your friends, get your horses and see me at the gates. GO!'

Kadis was very scared. He didn't have any idea of what was on his father's mind. But now it was beyond his control. King Rissho looked extremely agitated. Kadis had no choice but to obey his father's command.

◄§ 45 ২◙

A short while later, Kadis and his friends rode up to the massive gate. King Rissho looked stony-faced and didn't say anything when he saw Kadis and his friends ride up. He gestured for the big gates to be opened. With a loud grating noise, the huge gates slowly creaked open. It was an impressive sight but one that was lost on Kadis and his friends as they didn't know what lay ahead. The King and his General rode out of the gates majestically, followed by the Elite squad, with the young friends bringing up the rear.

The young soldiers of peace couldn't quite fathom what was going on in King Rissho's mind. If King Rissho attacked the peace party, then all their efforts would come to naught and things would not only go back to where they were but would probably be worse than before.

Kadis and his friends soon noticed the Molongan party in the distance – the peace party of King Toki, Princess Tara and their ministers. Slowly, the rival royal groups approached each other.

Then, facing each other, they stood still. It was like time had stopped. The only sounds were the heavy breathing of the horses and the blowing of the wind. The distance between them was short but the history they shared made it feel like they were a universe apart. King Toki made the first move. As he and Princess Tara got down from their carriage, King Toki's aide ran up with a silver tray full of gifts and offerings. Taking the tray with a smile, King Toki and Tara started to walk towards the King of Kofu. Fearing the worst, Kadis and his friends rode up to the front to join King Rissho. King Rissho dismounted from his horse. His General and the Commander of the Elite squad both walked up and stood on either side. King Rissho looked at the young friends with a stern expression and gestured to them to come stand beside him.

The two Kings with their core entourages walked slowly towards each other. Kadis looked nervously at his friends. He desperately wanted to plead with his father to accept peace. But, all the courage that the young Prince had gathered over the last few weeks was still not enough for him to do that.

Decades after the two royal leaders of Kofu and Molonga had stood facing each other in bitter conflict, on this windy and cloudy day the present-day Kings faced each other again. The two Kings stood silently looking at each other. Only a few days ago, the King of Molonga had been preparing to attack Kofu and bring it down to its knees. And the King of Kofu had been getting ready to defend his Kingdom and teach the Molongans a lesson they would never forget.

Breaking the silence, King Toki moved forward, and offered the tray to his royal cousin. 'Your Majesty, my cousin King Rissho, I offer this tray as a symbol of peace between our two Kingdoms. There's another carriage full of gifts behind me for you and your family. Though it can't match the offering you made us: the mystical sword that has been the symbol of pride for our side of the family for generations. The sword brought to us by your young son ... whom you sent into enemy territory to deliver it back to its rightful place ...'

Kadis and the others walked up to the two Kings and stood there meekly looking at their feet as no one spoke for a few moments. The only sound to be heard was the hum of the breeze. After what seemed like an eon, King Rissho finally spoke up. 'Today my son has made me a very proud man ...'

Kadis jerked his head up in surprise.

'What my son has accomplished with the help of his brave friends is very surprising and very impressive. I would never have thought they would be able to do what they did. And I am extremely pleased that you accepted this ... er ... offering of peace from us ...'

King Rissho looked at his son and gave him a cheeky wink, before continuing, '... and that they were safe and sound in your Kingdom.'

King Toki chuckled a bit at this statement.

'Well, not very safe in the dungeons of Molonga where they were imprisoned ... but as the saying goes, all's well that ends well!'

King Rissho cocked his eyebrow when he heard the word dungeon.

'*Dungeon?* You put my son in a *dungeon?*'

Kadis and his friends shut their eyes tight when they heard the King's change of tone. 'That's it,' Kadis thought, 'it's all over.'

King Toki continued even though Princess Tara tried to nudge him to stop. 'But your boy here and, of course, his friends, daringly escaped and somehow reached out to my daughter and told her why they were actually there ...'

'They ... they *escaped* from your dungeon?' asked King Rissho. He turned to look at his son and his friends. At first his face looked

grim, but a few moments later, a warm smile lit it up. 'You escaped from a dungeon? That's pretty brave of you, son!'

He then turned to his cousin, the King of Molonga, 'But they got out safe and sound and returned your sword to you. And here you are with gifts of peace. All's well that ends well indeed!'

King Rissho embraced King Toki. The two cousins and former enemies were locked in a tearful embrace for several moments.

Kadis and his friends jumped up in joy. In the distance, Kadis noticed a familiar horse carriage approaching. 'Granduncle Shonin!' he exclaimed happily.

Soon Shonin's carriage pulled up to the historic gathering. Kadis, Sara and Shijo ran up to greet him. The genial Shonin held them tight, feeling very proud of them. And then he walked up to the two Kings with a warm smile on his face – the smile of a family elder when he sees his young nephews, Kings or not.

King Rissho bowed respectfully and said, 'You're the one responsible for making this happen. Thank you, wise uncle Shonin. And an even bigger thank you for transforming my son into a brave Prince.'

'I'm no one to transform him ... the bravery was within him. It just had to be awakened ...'

King Toki went up to Shonin and affectionately embraced him. He then gestured to his aide who brought out the sword. It was now housed in a rich velvet case. He carefully drew it out. It had a radiant glow and looked as good as new. He looked at the sword for a few moments and then directly at Kadis. 'Son, please come here.'

Kadis walked up to Tara's father. As he bowed, he noticed

King Toki gesture to him to take the sword from his hands. Kadis looked towards his father who nodded, so he respectfully took the sword from the hands of King Toki. To everyone's surprise, it shone brightly the moment it touched the hands of the young Prince. King Toki smiled. 'Your Majesty, the legend has come true in front of our eyes. This brave young lad is The One. He was the one meant to bring peace between our families and Kingdoms. This sword belongs to him. I would like the honour of presenting this sword to the Prince of Kofu!'

King Rissho had tears in his eyes. This was the proudest moment of his life. The hearts of Shonin and all the others gathered there were filled with pride. King Toki continued, 'It would be our honour to merge Molonga with Kofu just like it used to be. I would be happy to just be the Governor of the State of Molonga, part of the bigger Kingdom of Kofu ... under the able rule of His Majesty King Rissho ...'

Everyone was stunned to hear King Toki make this magnanimous gesture. Overcome by emotion, King Rissho held his cousin in a tight embrace once again.

It was late afternoon. All of Kofu seemed to have gathered on the castle grounds. There was joy in the air. The King, Queen and Prince of Kofu sat on the podium outside the court, along with the nobility, and the most surprising presence of all – wise old Shonin, who hadn't been seen in Kofu for a long while. There were rumours that the war was over before it even began. Soon they would all know why.

King Rissho stood up to a roar of cheers. He raised his hand and the crowd fell silent.

'I have an announcement to make,' he began. 'Today I officially announce the cessation of hostilities between our Kingdom of Kofu and the neighbouring Kingdom of Molonga. While our army was preparing for war, my uncle Shonin and my son, the courageous Prince of Kofu, along with his very brave friends, went on a mission of peace.'

A murmur went through the crowd. King Rissho summoned Kadis and his brave friends.

'I present to you the young Prince of Kofu, and his best friends Shijo and Sara.'

The citizens gathered there applauded loudly.

King Rissho continued, 'Their mission was to enter Molonga, get an audience with His Highness King Toki and return the mystical sword, which was a symbol of the bad blood between the two Kingdoms. Their adventures will be chronicled soon and will be available for all to read. But, until then, all I can say is that under the able and wise guidance of Shonin the Wise, aided by the resourceful Mr. Joi, and with the support of the courageous Princess Tara and her companion Myo, they succeeded and came back safe and sound despite the many trials and tribulations. King Toki of Molonga got his family sword back and was convinced by these young soldiers to give peace a chance. And I am proud to say that he has.'

A hush fell over the crowd – the people couldn't believe what they were hearing.

'King Toki of Molonga met me in peace this morning, and we decided to start afresh. Not only that, but His Highness proposed that the two Kingdoms be merged just like they were before ... wherein it would still be called the Kingdom of Kofu. Molonga would go back to being its largest state with His Highness King Toki of Molonga as Governor.'

He looked at the surprised crowd as he addressed them.

'How do you think I responded?'

The people cheered unanimously,

'YES! YES!! YES!!!'

He raised his hands and the noise petered down.

'Well ... I REFUSED!'

This time the citizens didn't cheer. There was a buzz of confused voices and whispers. King Rissho looked at his aide and nodded. With a blast of trumpets King Toki of Molonga walked onto the podium. The citizens didn't know whether to applaud.

King Rissho walked up to welcome his cousin and then turned to address his citizens.

'King Toki has presented the mystical sword of his side of the family back to us. I have it here enclosed in a glass case for all to see!'

The sword lay in a glorious crystal case with gold edges and emitted a bright radiance.

'I have no words to tell you how I feel at this moment. With this gesture, His Highness has ended years of bitterness between us.'

He turned to his cousin.

'But I too have a proposal for you. I propose we break down the wall that separates us. And I also propose that you retain the Kingdom of Molonga and remain its King!'

This statement surprised everyone, most of all King Toki himself.

'Our Kingdoms can share borders ... where our people can freely travel to and fro, trade as one and be one people. But it would give me great pleasure to see you as His Highness, King of Molonga, a benevolent ruler from whom I too can learn. We will both be Kings ... equals who will work side by side for the happiness and benefit of the people of both Kingdoms. United, we will be an example for others, but still be even stronger than we are should someone from the outside even think of breaching that unity. We will be brothers again and our families will be one again!'

The roar of applause and cheering was almost deafening. No one had really wanted the war. No one really wanted to lose their loved ones for it.

Seeing King Rissho walk up to his son, the crowd became

quiet again. King Rissho smiled warmly as he noticed Kadis holding Sara's hand. 'I would also like to announce the betrothal of my son, Prince Kadis to Sara. Of course, with their permission! They will be married a few years from now – once they come of age.'

He turned with a loving smile towards Kadis and Sara. 'I hope that's all right with you both!'

Kadis looked shyly towards Sara. Sara couldn't contain her excitement and locked Kadis in a tight embrace. More cheers and applause followed.

King Rissho then went up to Shijo and Myo and winked at them. 'I would also like to announce the betrothal of young Shijo and Myo with their consent. They will get married alongside Prince Kadis and the future Princess Sara. Let this union be a symbol of the unity between our two Kingdoms!'

Myo covered her face shyly, beaming with happiness, while Shijo looked wide-eyed, as though this were a blissful dream.

King Rissho and Queen Kanito gracefully bowed to the citizens along with King Toki and Shonin. Princess Tara, Prince Kadis, Sara, Shijo, Myo and Mr. Joi bowed alongside. This was the happiest moment in the lives of all present there.

The sword shone brighter than it ever had before.

Kadis smiled as he thought to himself, 'The purpose of life is to be happy ourselves and help others become happy too. Why have war when we can have peace? The choice is *always* ours to make!'

Ruchi Shah is a book illustrator/wall artist. She is an alumnus of University of the Arts, London and IDC, IIT Bombay. She received the Charles Wallace Scholarship in 2012 through the British Council. Her works explore places, spaces, materials and stories of everyday life. After working in Yahoo as a senior designer, she quit in 2010 to work independently. She has illustrated more than 15 books that have been published multilingually. Some of her works include *Our Incredible Cow* and *Candid Tales*. She also facilitates art workshops across different regions of India and Uganda. She received British Council's Social Impact Award in 2018 for her work.

Jugal Hansraj is a film actor, writer and National Award-winning film director, originally from Mumbai, India. He began working in films first as a child actor – *Masoom (1983)* being the most notable. He then went on to become a lead actor in films like *Papa Kahte Hain (1996)* and *Mohabbattein (2000)* among others. In 2006 he turned writer-director and made the animation film *Roadside Romeo (2008)* and in 2010 he directed the feature film *Pyaar Impossible!* He's still seen on screen as an actor at regular intervals. His first book as author, *Cross Connection – The Big Circus Adventure*, was published in 2017. *The Coward & The Sword* is his second novel. He is currently based in New York.

Acknowledgements

There are some people I wish to thank:

My family – my late father for always encouraging my creative side; my late mother for all the love and blessings that I am eternally grateful for; my beautiful wife Jasmine who is also my truest friend and my lifeline; my son Sidak, my reason to smile every moment and my inspiration to write; my older brother Sunil for his constant support and for always standing by me like a rock; my niece Shalini, the first person to read my complete manuscript and showering me with her encouraging words.

My friends Tushar Menon and Paras Ghelani for taking the time out of their busy lives to review my manuscript and giving me their very valuable feedback which helped make this a better book.

Mr. Shambhu Sahu of Words Count Editorial for having faith in my writing, for instantly agreeing to represent me and for taking my manuscript to HarperCollins India.

Ms. Tina Narang and the entire team at HarperCollins India. Having this book published by HarperCollins is an absolute honour and the team was a pleasure to interact with.

The late Mr. Joe Sheth, my English Language/Literature in English teacher at Campion School, Mumbai, for instilling in me a profound love for books and an appreciation for the mysteries of the English language.

े